FOLLIES HOTEL

When Julianne's engagement ring goes missing and her love letters disappear, she is distraught. Then she hears that her beloved fiancé, the Earl of Featherstonhaugh, is involved in scandal. When he stops writing to her, Julianne decides she must find out what has happened. She goes to his London house and discovers the embarrassing reason . . . Can their true love overcome the difficulty?

ANNE HOLMAN

FOLLIES HOTEL

Complete and Unabridged

LINFORD
Leicester

First published in Great Britain in 2010

First Linford Edition
published 2010

British Library CIP Data

Holman, Anne, *1934* –
　　Follies Hotel.- -(Linford romance library)
　　1. Aristocracy (Social class)- -England- -
　　London- -Fiction. 2. Scandals- -Fiction.
　　3. Love stories. 4. Large type books.
　　I. Title II. Series
　　823.9'2–dc22

ISBN 978–1–44480–412–6

Published by
F. A. Thorpe (Publishing)
Anstey, Leicestershire

Set by Words & Graphics Ltd.
Anstey, Leicestershire
Printed and bound in Great Britain by
T. J. International Ltd., Padstow, Cornwall

This book is printed on acid-free paper

1

Nicholas, Earl of Featherstonhaugh, raised his fine looking features to look at his land agent, Mr Crossley, who stood politely by his desk. 'Have we dealt with everything now?' he asked.

'Yes, m'lord . . . except . . . I don't know if you've heard about . . . '

Tapping his long fingers on the accounts book, Nicholas breathed deeply, and waited to hear what Crossley was so reluctant to tell him about.

Nothing, he thought, could be worse than what he'd suffered recently. His father had died leaving him with a mountain of debts. He'd inherited a country mansion needing urgent repairs. His younger brother, Jack, seemed to be going the way of his father and was sent down from Oxford for excessive gambling.

Worst of all, a week ago his beautiful, adorable fiancée, Julianne Appleby, had sent back his engagement ring.

'Come on, man, spit it out. More debts have come to light, eh?'

Mr Crossley spoke quietly, 'No, m'lord. It concerns a tit-bit the ton gossips have been spreading around town.'

Nicholas gave a pressed lipped smile.

It didn't take much to scandalise some members of High Society.

'Well, that's no change!' he said, 'they never stop spreading scandal. What have they been saying this time?'

'It concerns Viscount Milverton.'

The Earl's smile disappeared immediately hearing his brother's name.

Mr Crossley gave a little cough. Then he enquired, 'Didn't his lordship inform you about the Follies Hotel?'

Nicholas groaned. 'No, he did not.'

Where his brother, Jack, was concerned anything scandalous was possible. That included everything the word 'follies' suggested. Unwise conduct and frivolity bordering on stupidity seemed to be enjoyable to that irrepressible young dandy.

Circulating scandal was fun to hear about except when it concerned you or your family. Nicholas was afraid anything he heard that was to do with Jack probably would not amuse him. Not that Nicholas didn't like his brother; indeed he did. He even secretly envied Jack his carefree ways. His life wasn't in the least dull, like his was at the moment.

Of course, Jack didn't have the responsibilities of the Featherstonhaugh estates as he had. Nicholas felt shackled to them, thinking of the burden of his father's debts, which, although he was slowly paying them off, seemed intolerable at times.

He disliked how draughty and cold the big house had become over the past freezing winter months when he could not afford to heat it properly. Featherstonhaugh Hall, with its sparse fires to warm the huge rooms did indeed make it seem as if he was in the Antarctic.

And he missed company — especially his dearest Julianne. On more than one occasion he'd almost felt tempted to simply sell up and emigrate — with Julianne, of course.

But now Julianne seemed to want to desert him!

Rising to his six foot height, revealing his perfectly cut country wear and neatly tied cravat, the Earl pounded over the library floorboards towards one of the long sash windows.

He gazed out over the vast green lawns and shimmering lake where two swans glided in the spring sunshine. He was fond of the place and didn't really want to sell it. He'd had a happy childhood at Featherstonhaugh Hall until his sensible mama had died, and his profligate papa was left in charge.

' . . . the viscount is making a good profit from it.'

Nicholas became aware that Mr Crossley was still talking to him and swung around. 'Did I hear you say, profit?'

'Yes indeed, m'lord. I have heard tell that the Follies Hotel is making a great deal of money.'

'Well, I'll be jiggered!' He'd underestimated his brother's business acumen. Perhaps he could learn some money-making tricks from Jack!

On second thoughts Nicholas could count on it that the way Jack filled up his coffers would not be considered at all proper. Hence, all the whisperings going around the beau mode.

However, Nicholas was curious. 'I must see this hotel for myself,' he said. 'Where is it situated?'

'It's in Mayfair, m'lord. It's your town house, actually.'

Nicholas's eyes widened as he bellowed, 'Do you mean my brother has turned my town house into a hotel?'

'Indeed, m'lord. It's a very private and discreet hotel — and a very popular one by all accounts.'

But not private or discreet enough evidently. Now Nicholas could understand what the gossip was all about!

His ancestors would be haunting him forever. Imagine, allowing strangers into the elegant interior of his fine town house!

He pictured his mama's carved and gilt beechwood couch in cerise upholstery being used in her drawing room. People he didn't know sitting on the Hepplewhite chairs in the striped wallpapered dining room. And Lord knows what was going on in the many bedrooms!

No wonder the family reputation was being shredded — and his sweet Julianne must have heard about it and had ended her engagement to him by sending his ring back.

It was partly his own fault of course, a result of his lack of judgement. He'd thoughtlessly given his brother his town house to look after while he'd been away from London trying to sort out the mess he'd been left with on the neglected estates.

The last thing he envisaged while he was gone was that his fashionable address in Mayfair would be turned into a gaming den!

But Nicholas was more than a little curious to know exactly what was going on there — before he threw everyone out, of course! He gave a chuckle. Although his own rakish days were over, he suddenly felt a strong desire to indulge in a little night life. It would make a break from ploughing through the dreary accounts.

Jack, he knew, had a taste for fine wine, women and song and he had to admire his younger brother for actually making some golden guineas at last, instead of losing them.

A gurgle of mirth surged up from his throat, and his explosive laughter made Mr Crossley hastily make towards the door.

'Stay awhile and tell me more about this profitable folly of my brother's,' Nicholas begged his agent. He decided that he might as well know the worst of the situation — after all, he could hardly undo what had already been done, but he may well have to try to rectify it.

★ ★ ★

Later that day Nicholas received a letter from his aunt, Lady Bridget:

My dear Nicholas,

I have just heard with great dismay that you have broken your promise to marry my Goddaughter, Julianne Appleby.

As both a great friend and sister-in-law of your darling mama, I know she would be appalled. She told me you two were made for each other. Julianne was over the moon when she became engaged to you and now the poor girl is most upset.

I trust this must be only a lovers' tiff that should be healed immediately. Remember dear boy, Julianne is an heiress, and you are not in a financial position that makes it sensible to cast her aside.

Nicholas rubbed his jaw savagely. Damn it all, it was she who sent my ring back! It was Julianne who decided to stop our correspondence, not me!

Continuing to read, he became alarmed:

Therefore, because I care for you both, I have decided to invite, Julianne to my town house for the coming Season. You would do well to bury your pride and offer to escort her.

We arrive on Tuesday and will be calling on you at the earliest opportunity.

Your loving aunt,

Bridget.

Nicholas glanced at the date on the letter and gave a groan. Would he be able to get to his town house to clear out Jack and his hotel guests before the ladies arrived?

He also needed to see his beloved Julianne and talk to about why she had sent his ring back and why she had not answered his recent letters.

He was sure she loved him, so what had made her change her mind? Had she met another man she wished to marry? Surely not — they were promised to each other. Nothing could break the love they had for each other, certainly not a ridiculous bit of scandal!

He felt sure Julianne had far more sense than to send her ring back because of Jack's antics.

It was his own fault, of course, for putting off going to see her, he should have done so as soon as he received his ring. But he'd been too surprised, too hurt, to doing anything at first. He'd felt too upset to ask her and had felt that she should have sent a message to explain why she'd done it.

But now he knew he must abandon his affairs at Featherstone Hall and go immediately to find out what had happened. He must confront Julianne and sort out the problem.

He didn't want to lose the girl he loved — and it didn't have anything to do with her fortune. He was confident he had now sorted out his own finances sufficiently well and could now support a wife.

Calling his valet to pack his travel bag and his groom to saddle his fastest horse — he could no longer afford to run the family coach — Nicholas prepared to leave Featherstonhaugh Hall. He must get to his London house as soon as possible, at least before his aunt arrived there.

2

It was a fine spring day, with the leaves of the town trees unfolding bright green in the sunshine, as Julianne looked anxiously out of the carriage making its way towards Mayfair. Easing back the window curtain with her gloved hand she enjoyed the thrill of seeing as much as possible of bustling London life. But she felt immediately sad when she was reminded she was not wearing her beloved's engagement ring.

It had been a mystery to her what had happened to it.

At the end of the London Season last year, she'd been told by her fiancé, Nicholas, the Earl of Featherstonhaugh, that his father had died. He requested an extended betrothal because he needed time to sort out his estate's business, which he'd explained were left to him in dire straights. So Julianne accepted she'd have to wait a long time before her marriage.

She regretted it but she told herself that it was no worse for any young lady whose husband was a soldier who had to go off and fight wars. Or it would be the same as being engaged to a trader who had to go abroad for a spell. She knew she would just have to be patient.

Anyway, she felt that it would make no difference to her how long she had to wait for him. Nicholas was the only man she would ever love and want to marry.

Therefore, she was devastated in the New Year when her mother explained to her that his long absence and the lack of correspondence from him meant that his lordship regretted their coming union, and Julianne should accept that he had changed his mind.

Julianne had protested bitterly, crying out, 'I simply cannot believe that!'

Mrs Clara Appleby, who was sitting in her elegant lounge and tinkering on her harpsichord, said, 'My dear, broken engagements are preferable to marrying the wrong man.'

'But I love Nicholas, Mama.'

'I dare say you do — that is, you did. Most young gels can count on having a passion for some man or other before they get married. But now I think you should understand your first love affair is over.'

Julianne knew she could hardly blame her mother if the Earl had indeed decided to be done with her. The truth was they'd had little opportunity to spend time together.

Meeting during her first Season and falling in love in the staid atmosphere of Society's strictly conventional functions had given them only a brief opportunity to show their passionate love for each other. And despite the warmth of their private correspondence it had now ceased and he hadn't given her any indication as to why.

She was puzzled that Nicholas had not had the good manners to do so. All his faults — which had been not been mentioned previously by her social-climbing mama after she'd captured an Earl to marry — were now suddenly revealed by her mama, who was keen to say how unacceptable Nicholas was for her to marry.

Although some of the tales about his youthful follies amused Julianne, some did not, but she still considered Nicholas to be a man of honour who, she hoped, still loved her.

No, she decided, he couldn't have jilted her.

'Mama,' she said, as her mother stretched her fingers over the keyboard playing a Chopin piece, 'I don't know why he has offered me no explanation. It is not like Nicholas to — '

'My dear child, he doesn't have to tell you why. You only have to listen to what everyone is saying about him. He will take it for granted that you will want to call off your engagement.'

Startled, Julianne took in a sharp breath and blurted out, 'I haven't heard any malicious gossip about him from my friends.'

'No, you wouldn't have. I dare say they are too kind to tell you about his latest escapade.'

For the first time Julianne felt her heart tumble down to her pumps. With a trembling voice she asked, 'What escapade?'

Her mama finished her playing with a flourish and, leaving her hands in the air, turned with a haughty look at her daughter, saying, 'I'm sure you do not need to hear exactly what the Earl is tangled up with. But I've heard from an impeccable source that, just as he was a rake as a young man, he is now engaged in some exceedingly improper conduct. I do not want you besmirched by it. So he will understand if you take off his ring.'

Julianne raised her delicate left hand and looked down at the ring, sparkling with diamonds set in a cluster of three raised silver clasps that he had told her represented his heart, her heart, and his heir that they were going to produce together. It represented the whole purpose of her life: to love and be loved, and to produce a child.

'No, Mama! I will not take off his ring!' she cried.

'But my dear child, you must understand your betrothal is over!'

Defiantly Julianne raised her voice, 'It is not over, Mama. I think about Nicholas every day. I will not put him out of my mind.'

'Stuff and nonsense! The Earl of Featherstonhaugh has inherited nothing but debts from his father and has been paying them off by trading in a most indecorous manner. Your papa would not approve of that.'

How did she know her deceased papa would not approve?

Her memories of her dear father, Mr Appleby, was that he was a fun-loving man. He'd made an enormous fortune from his jewellery business and left half of it to her. No doubt, before he died, he wished his daughter to have the freedom to enjoy her life, well aware of his wife's shrivelled sense of humour and her inability to see beyond the narrow straits of what Society approved of. Julianne was sure he would want her to gain all she could from what the world had to offer. And that included making up her own mind about who she should marry.

Her mother's scolding continued, 'I would prefer you married a pauper, than be utterly ruined in the eyes of Society by marrying that Earl with his utterly disgraceful behaviour.'

What disgraceful behaviour? Julianne refrained from saying she should be told about it and allowed to decide for herself if it was so.

Having her own fortune, what did it matter if she married an impoverished aristocrat? Anyway, she doubted the Earl and she would ever starve to death, however poor her mama thought they would be. And as for Society's dictates, good gracious me, wasn't being a countess more that enough to prevent her from being considered a social outcast?

However, she began to worry when the letters from Nicholas that she treasured so much ceased arriving. She'd tied the ones she had with a scarlet ribbon and stored them with his ring — which she'd had to remove from her finger eventually to save her mother from nagging her — and she'd put them in a silk purse in her dressing table drawer.

But one day when Julianne went to look at them, the purse had gone!

She looked everywhere for her engagement ring and her love letters, but couldn't find them. The hue and cry she made could be heard all over the house — and probably in the local village, too. The servants were questioned, windows and shutter fasteners were checked, but no clue to a burglar entering the house could be found.

'You probably sent the purse to the laundry with your washing by mistake,' her mother suggested, then added cruelly, 'but as you are finished with him it does not really matter.'

But it did matter to Julianne. She was devastated. She still loved him; he occupied her mind all the time. He always would, no matter that her mama believed that him making her wait so long to marry him showed he wasn't returning her love. And what did she care about him being engaged in some sort of improper business until she knew the facts?

Then, depending what he was up to, she might decide he was not, after all, for her. But how could that possibly be?

She remembered when she first saw him it was like being struck by lightning. She knew immediately he was the man for her. Oh, indeed, she had been told he was a rake, that she should beware of him — but didn't that just make him all the more exciting to know?

His smile — as if he knew her already — sent shivers through her.

And after they were introduced, what

did she care when she discovered he was a man of high birth? It was his assured nature, good looks and impeccable manners that attracted her. Indeed, he told her he'd been smitten in the same way she had. They chose to be together whenever they could. They'd laughed happily throughout last Season's diversions.

They'd danced the waltz together while she looked lovingly up into his gloriously deep blue and intelligent eyes that promised so many delights ahead for them to enjoy together.

But now, as the carriage trundled over the cobblestones into Mayfair on that glorious spring morning she was only partly able to enjoy it as she wondered if some other fortunate girl had captured Nicholas's heart.

Maybe she had to accept that she'd lost him? That's why she had come to London, to find out. When her kindly Godmother, Lady Bridget, had insisted she accompany her to London for the Season, it was just the opportunity she needed.

Her mother had instructed her before she left home that she must look for another man to marry. Reclining on her sofa bed, Mama had fanned herself saying, 'I can no longer stand the rigours of Society. Your Godmother, Lady Bridget, enjoys the theatre, balls, assemblies and card parties and she is happy to chaperone you.'

Mentioning those social occasions, Julianne knew she would enjoy them and anticipating going to London brightened her expression.

Mrs Appleby continued, 'You'll be a little older than most gels coming out this year, but you'll still be the finest catch this Season. And with your new wardrobe of gowns to enhance your perfect figure and golden hair, you'll have no difficulty in selecting from the best of the eligible gentlemen.'

Although Julianne wasn't intending to shop for a husband, she didn't say so. Arguing with her mother was useless. She knew she had to appear to agree with whatever her mother said until she came of age.

But Miss Julianne Appleby knew just getting away from her dominating and socially ambitious mother for a spell would be a blessing.

Her mama hadn't finished her instructions yet, and told her, 'By the way, if you should meet Earl Featherstonhaugh in London, he won't do more than bow to acknowledge you and that is all you need do yourself.'

* * *

So, although Julianne wanted Nicholas more than any other man on earth, she dreaded meeting him. She had to find out what he was up to, and decide for herself if she still wanted to marry him. She was relieved that for most of the day she'd be wearing long kid gloves and, she hoped, he may not notice the missing ring.

But fearing the Earl was no fool and might ask her why she was not wearing it, she thought she could always explain that she had mislaid it, perhaps even suggesting that it had slipped off her finger because she'd lost weight pining for him! In fact she dreamed up many excuses for explaining why she didn't have his ring on her finger, but hoped he'd believe the truth, that she'd simply mislaid it.

On the other hand, she may find, as her mama had said, that he had truly gone to the devil during the past few winter months and she no longer liked him after he'd been away wintering at Featherstonehaugh Hall. Although she felt sure this was unlikely.

But the joy of seeing him again and having the chance of being in his company, or better still dancing in his arms, was unbearably exciting! Needing to confront him, Julianne had decided to brave the London Season and so, here she was in London, full of apprehension and approaching the disgraced bear's lair.

She could see the good sense in her

going to his house as soon as possible but, unfortunately, she felt her stomach turning somersaults. But why should she feel disturbed? He was the one at fault by not writing to her.

It was Lady Bridget who'd persuaded her to visit Nicholas at home on their first day in town before they did anything else.

Her ladyship had spoken to her firmly, 'My dear nephew, Nicholas, is a good natured and kind man. But he can be difficult, even in the wrong, at times. Most men can be. It's a woman's job to manage them. What has happened between you two I don't wish to know, but I am sure it is nothing more than a bumblebroth.'

'So you must get this difficult meeting with him over, Julianne. Straighten out your differences without delay. The sooner you tame the beast, the sooner we can get on with enjoying a full programme of entertainments.'

Easier said than done, thought Julianne, thinking of the lofty Earl with his commanding ways. She went over every detail she remembered about how they had crept away into their hostess's garden one warm evening last Season, when her chaperone had been engaged in talking to another and not noticed her slip off hand-in-hand with Nicholas.

Oh, he had easily managed to move her out of sight of the music room where the contralto was entertaining the rest of the guests with German love songs. Once hidden by some bushes, his gentle kisses had become more passionate and her control of his desires lessened quickly as his tender hands soothed her lovingly and his contented breathing was interjected with him saying, 'I love you, my adorable Julianne.'

She just wanted the delicious feeling to continue and never stop but he said suddenly, 'We must go back!'

'Why?' she asked in a delightful dizzy daze.

Then he told her how he really

wanted to stay, but until she had accepted his proposal of marriage, he would not harm her reputation by lingering outside alone with her.

'But I want to marry you,' she'd cried.

'That I hope is true, my dear. But we must do things properly. You must have time to consider. We have only known each for a few months. Marriage is a lifetime commitment. Your mama must be considered too,' he said tenderly squeezing her hand before letting it go.

'But Nicholas. I already know I want to marry you.'

'I'm truly honoured that you do, my dearest, but I too have to take time to consider. I have to prepare myself to be a good husband and father.'

Coming out of her rapture, Julianne knew he was right. He was being honourable and considerate, and she admired that.

Walking back to join the assembly, she felt proud to have the love of a man who was promising to be true to her, as she would always be to him.

But those blessed memories of enjoying being with him were in the past.

What, Julianne wondered, was in the future for them both?

3

Nicholas had travelled fast for three days. He'd stopped overnight at post inns to have a meal and get a fresh horse — and to avoid highwaymen, because he carried Julianne's ring and did not want it stolen.

His fine clothes were muddied by the time he arrived at his London house early in the morning, just as a big delivery cart arrived and blocked his way into the mews.

As the grooms were dealing with the great shire horses that pulled the cart, he was obliged to dismount and walk his sweat-covered horse around to cool the animal down before tethering it to a lamp-post.

He needed to cool himself down, too. Not being able to get into his own property inflamed his temper.

Hearing the delivery men arguing as

to the best way to get a large statue off their cart and move it into the house made him edge nearer to observe. The statue was of a near naked woman that was only just acceptable because it was an example of classical nudity.

'Good Lord!' His curiosity got the better of him as he strained to get a better look at the female form.

'Get orf, out the way with you!' one of the men, staggering under the weight of the big piece of sculpture, spat at him.

Grasping his riding whip tightly Nicholas was about to put the man straight about who he was talking to when he saw the man trip and had to act quickly to prevent the statue from landing on the cobblestones and smashing into dozens of fragments.

He grasped hold of the heavy object and was surprise to find just how weighty a lump of marble was. But to a chorus of advice being shouted by the other removal men, he and they finally transported the stone woman through the kitchen and into the hall.

'Whew! That was a near one. Thank ye kindly for your help,' the grimy faced furniture remover smiled at the Earl. Then, noting his fine riding apparel, the man added, 'Sir.'

'Bring it over here — careful now — it's going under the stairs.' Nicholas heard his brother, Jack, giving instructions.

Nicholas felt like countermanding that order and having it thrown out of the house. But did he really want such an indelicate item put outside his house, for all to see? He would have to let it stay for now but would soon have it taken away. Or could he use it to adorn the garden at Featherstonhaugh Hall? It might suit there as there were already many near naked figurines along the garden paths.

It had been, he considered, as he looked again at the statue, created by a modern sculptor. He liked the skilled carving of the drapery falling over the stone curves of the woman — for some reason it reminded him of his fiancée, sweet Julianne.

Which reminded him of why he'd come to London in the first place — to prevent his fiancée and aunt from being exposed to this kind of display of Jack's choice of decorative sculpture. Wondering what to do about it he stood in the hall in a quandary.

'Nicholas, old boy,' he heard Jack say, as he received a hearty thump on the back, 'what a surprise to see you here!'

Nicholas turned to look at his brother but could barely see Jack's face behind his extraordinary stand up winged collar. His fashionable dandy style jacket had a pinched in waist and his close fitting pantaloons revealed as much about his figure as any risque statue!

Before Nicholas could think of something suitable to say to the reprobate, Jack had his arm around his shoulders saying, 'I consider you need the attentions of my valet. I'll ring for him.' Jack strode over to a bell pull saying, 'Strewth, Nicholas, I've never seen you look so bedraggled.'

'Jack!' boomed Nicholas who'd had the time to glance around and see more of the décor with its bright red tasselled curtains, crimson velvet sofas and several pictures which were related in subject matter to the statue he had helped cart in. 'What have you done to my house?'

'Don't put yourself in a tweak. I've only modernised the house a little. Now do go upstairs and partake of a bath. You are, dare I mention it, the most disreputable thing in the whole house — and you stink of horse! Now off you go upstairs. I'll tell the servants to bring up several ewers of hot water.'

Realising that he did badly need to bathe and change, and therefore feeling at a disadvantage to begin to demonstrate with his brother, the Earl of Featherstonhaugh stamped up the broad staircase, trying not to notice the new pictures on the walls or look at the lush furnishings which had changed considerably since his parents resided there.

The attentive valet was waiting for him and was delighted to show him to his bedroom where he saw a new bathtub with cherubs painted on the outside. While Nicholas stripped and stood waiting to get into the tub the valet filled it with the hot water brought into the bedroom by a clutch of maids — Maids? He grabbed a bath towel and quickly slid behind the dressing screen. But the maids didn't appear to be in the least worried about his state of undress. One young minx had the audacity to whisper to another and they giggled as they left the room.

The valet then produced assorted bottles of intriguingly coloured bath oils and perfumes for Nicholas to choose from. Nicholas protested they were far in excess of his normal manly soap. But a dollop of something bright green and fragrant was put in the water before he got into the tub.

Later, with his face shaved, hair cut

and combed, and a freshly laundered set of clothes on, Nicholas felt surprisingly and delightfully pampered. He was more in control of himself, too, and was ready to go downstairs and put Jack in his place.

Running down the stairs he was soon put out of sorts again by meeting a saucy maid who winked at him. She was carrying a tray with what appeared to be someone's breakfast on it. Who else was in the house, he wondered? I must find Jack and get this duced-odd situation stopped at once.

Walking across the hall he met the aged butler, Biggs, he recognised from his youth and decided he must have a word with him too. But before Nicholas could ask the man a question the butler said in a stiff, high-toned voice as he bowed, 'Your lordship, I have just seen Lady Bridget's carriage drive up. Shall I show her ladyship into the saloon?'

His first reaction was to tell the man to say that he was not at home, but Lady Bridget was his favourite aunt. If anyone could help him out of the hole he was in, it was she.

'Show her in Biggs. I'll deal with her myself,' he said wondering where on earth would be a safe place to take her. As it was a pleasant morning the garden might be somewhere he could hide her away from Jack's idea of modern refurbishment, but he doubted if Jack would have spared even the garden from more statues of doubtful respectability.

Too late anyway — he heard Aunt Bridget saying, 'Thank you Biggs. Take our bonnets, if you please. Now where's my nephew?'

'Whom do you wish to see, m'lady?'

'Why, Earl Featherstonhaugh, of course. It's his house isn't it?'

At that precise moment Nicholas wished he could say it was not. Although he hoped he would have the opportunity to ask his aunt to help him to persuade Jack to restore the house to its former old-fashioned and respectable state.

What he didn't expect was that, when her ladyship entered the house, she would have his erstwhile fiancée in tow.

★   ★   ★

Julianne's eyes rested on the tall Earl and she found he was even more handsome than she had remembered — and yet he hadn't changed a bit. His features were extremely pleasing, if a little hawkish at the moment because he didn't look exactly pleased to see her. One eyebrow had risen slightly higher than the other but that was only to be expected as he, like she, must be wondering how this encounter might end and affect their future lives.

He bowed to his aunt and kissed her on both cheeks, while Julianne, remembering her mama's advice, stood well back and curtsied to him prettily. She would have smiled, only she was a little afraid of what he might say or do if she did.

He smiled at her though, a slightly

wolfish smile she thought. It may have been intended to fox her, but she actually found it quite delicious.

'My dear Aunt Bridget, and Julianne, welcome to my — the — house.'

Bridget cast a look around and said in her low voice, 'Can't say you've improved the hall since you've inherited it, Nicholas.'

'As you say, Aunt,' Nicholas waved a dismissive hand, 'it does need a few alterations here and there.'

His aunt looked at the newly installed statue under the staircase and said dryly. 'Many, I would suggest. I would start by getting rid of that female statue. Whatever made you put it there? You mama always had a palm tree under the stairs, so much nicer than that . . . ' she clearly found the statue difficult to describe and it was clear she didn't approve of it.

'Yes, Aunt,' said Nicholas nodding

Julianne was still admiring her fiancé. His beautifully cut amethyst-coloured morning coat and expertly tied cravat couldn't be bettered. My goodness, she thought, his prolonged stay in the country hadn't allowed any weeds to grow over him. He's glowing with perfect health. It's a shame he doesn't appear perfectly happy.

Aunt Bridget put Julianne's thoughts into words when she said, 'I can see you are in a pucker, Nicholas. Forgive this unannounced early morning visit, but I considered there was an urgent matter between you two lovebirds to be discussed forthwith.'

That statement didn't make him look any happier. In fact, Julianne thought, examining him more closely, the poor Earl looked somewhat harassed and vulnerable.

Perhaps it was having his aunt thrust 'an urgent matter' at him so early in the morning. After all, he may have been up most of the night, gambling, drinking, doing the things most gentlemen did in the evenings, and was not expecting them quite so early. Although Lady Bridget had told her he had been informed that she would call on him without delay when she'd arrive in London. Maybe appearing so soon after break of day had interfered with some other engagement he had in mind that morning. She just hoped it was not with another woman.

She continued to gaze starry-eyed at him as he chatted to his aunt, and she then noticed the statue behind his head. She was mildly shocked at the female's pose. It was certainly not one she'd been taught at her ladies seminary. But she couldn't help quite liking the artist's skilled work, although she could understand why her mama wouldn't.

'Julianne.' Hearing her name she panicked and realised the Earl was approaching her, making her suddenly feel like running under the stairs and hiding behind the great sculpture.

'Nicholas,' she managed to say, feeling a blush sweep over her neck and face. How she disliked being scrutinised so closely by him, even though she had chosen her outfit with care that morning and knew that her hair was dressed beautifully.

Why was he was looking at her with disapproval, as if she was an errant child? Perhaps she shouldn't have come? Perhaps he hoped their love affair was over because he had found another woman he preferred to her? Perhaps by not writing to her he'd hoped she would understand their engagement was over?

'Julianne, you look charming, my dear,' he said, his spontaneous smile dispelling any thoughts she had about not being welcome. So all was well. Then she remembered she didn't have his ring on her finger and it made her afraid her hammering heart could be heard.

He held out his well-shaped hand to take hers and he appeared surprised she didn't offer it. Seeming not in the least nonplussed he smoothly lowered his face to press his lips on hers with a firm kiss that made her jump.

'You are more than welcome, Julianne, my dear,' he said in a voice that sent a sensation like a fluttering moth down her spine.

Keeping her hands firmly behind her back Julianne felt like a caged bird, wanting to fly away, wondering how she'd ever agreed to marry a man quite so strong-minded like him. He was frighteningly dynamic.

However, deep in her heart she knew she still loved him. Passionately.

But the real question was: did he still love her?

Meanwhile Aunt Bridget had been wandering around the hall looking at the pictures, 'Can't say I like your taste in these either,' she declared.

'Oh, Aunt, I regret you are no connoisseur!' Jack's voice boomed as he strolled into the hall and gave an exaggerated low bow to the lady and then to Julianne, who was amazed to find the Earl's brother so like him.

Indeed, Julianne was much struck by seeing another handsome gentleman and Jack looked so pleased to see her. He seemed so good-humoured and fun and extremely fashionably dressed.

'These pictures are the work of an émigré,' Jack informed his aunt, 'a French painter who came to work in London to escape from Napoleon.'

Julianne heard Nicholas mutter, 'He would run away from me, too, if I got anywhere near him.'

Amused, Julianne was alarmed again when she heard Jack say, 'I'm sure Julianne approves of all the new art we have here.'

All eyes turned on her. Finding her opinion requested, Julianne's eyelashes fluttered as she turned to examine the nearest picture. *It is just as well I am already blushing*, she thought. *The work is . . . really, I can't put words to what I think about what I am seeing, but my face is all aflush.*

She thought fleetingly that the Earl might be enjoying her confusion but fortunately he came gallantly to her rescue.

'These pictures may be a little too modern for Julianne. Now, my dear,' he said kindly, offering her his hand, which she refused again, so he slipped his arm gently around her waist and led her towards the dining room, 'I expect, you would like some refreshment, dearest. I can see you are a trifle warm. It will be cooler in the dining room.'

Yes, indeed, she felt hot. His closeness, his body brushing close to hers, his fingers around her waist, together with his scent, accounted for her fiery glow of pleasure.

'Thank you, my lord, I do feel a trifle fatigued.' She struggled to know what to say to hide her disorder, 'I only travelled from home yesterday, and I'm not yet used to being in amongst the busy London town life.'

'I understand. I've only just arrived here myself, having ridden from the country,' he explained soothingly, 'I feel in need a muffin and a dish of coffee before I start dealing with my aunt's urgent problems or, indeed, with anything else that has to be sorted out.'

4

Nicholas might have known the furnishing in the dining room would make a statement as risqué as the rest of the house, but as Jack's intention had been to make it so and its impact had already been made on the ladies what could he do about it, except bluff his way through?

Aunt Bridget had been talking to Jack when she suddenly became aware of her surroundings.

'Nicholas,' she said severely, 'I thought you had changed your ways!' She pointed to a piece of Greek pottery where near naked men were depicted chasing almost naked girls. 'Just look at that decorative border, it leaves nothing at all to the imagination.'

'It's classical art — or a copy of it,' Nicholas informed her in a bid to defend the object's lack of propriety.

'Surely you know that the classical mode is all the fashion these days? That vase is just one example of how the Greeks adorned their houses.'

'And they were not at all squeamish about what they got up to in those houses either,' Jack added wickedly.

'They may not have been,' Aunt Bridget declared icily, 'but one does not need to be reminded of it first thing in the morning!'

Fortunately, at that moment, Biggs came in followed by a string of other servants bearing trays with jugs of steaming coffee and great silver domed platters, which they placed on the side table.

Soon the visitors were being brought cups of coffee from the maids, who seemed unusually chirpy and anxious to please.

As the party was served and started to partake of their refreshments, Nicholas guessed why Julianne, who looked so desirable in her lilac-sprigged gown and her hair piled up but with curled ringlets falling either side of her face, also looked uncomfortable — she was trying to keep her left hand out of sight.

'Have you hurt your hand, my dear?' he asked with an innocent smile as he leant over to whisper in her ear. They were able to talk privately since his aunt and Jack were engaged in discussing a framed portrait of a young shepherd caressing a shepherdess.

'No, Nicholas, I regret to say that I . . . ' Julianne coloured more brightly as she gabbled on quickly, explaining about having somehow mislaid his ring that morning. He thought it not, only amusing but deceitful of her to say she'd lost his ring when she'd sent it back to him some time ago — and he had it this very minute in his pocket.

Nicholas gave a quiet sigh. Just as his brother, Jack, had filled his town house with doubtfully respectable art follies, Julianne was playing an equally amusing game about losing his ring, wasn't she?

Well, he could soon deal with Jack and his art follies after his aunt and

Julianne had gone. Throwing them all out of his house was a relatively easy matter. But dealing with Julianne wasn't going to be as easy because, although he knew she was lying to him, he still loved and wanted her.

His interest — amusement really — in Julianne's deceit was only partial. Despite it being before noon he was feeling he wanted to kiss her flushed cheeks as he admired her slender neck and the swell of her bosom. How lovely she was. He had every intention of sorting out the teasing game she was playing because he still intended to marry her.

★ ★ ★

Julianne was fast overcoming her sense of surprise bordering on mild outrage at being surrounded by the display of art that portrayed love so openly and so basely.

Who was she thinking of marrying? Had Nicholas so little sense of propriety, filling his house with such things?

Would she really want to live in a house decorated like this? What would her friends think, let alone Society?

Now she understood what her mother had been referring to about his lapse of decorous behaviour.

The house was obviously full of such objets d'art, some of which, like her Godmother had said, went a little beyond the limits of respectable adornment. She was intrigued to know why Nicholas thought he needed such things in his house.

But she was also puzzled because he didn't seem to defend having them by saying he liked them, or how good the artists who made them were, like Jack did. In fact, she had the distinct feeling Nicholas didn't like most of them any more than she did. So why had he installed them?

Now his handsome, charming brother, Jack, was a different kind of man. He was amusing, more straightforward than Nicholas, saying he liked the art work. Julianne felt she knew where she stood with him, even though she didn't share his taste in ultra modern clothes and the house décor.

Suddenly the dining room door was flung open and a flushed young lady entered followed by an equally flushed young man.

'I say, Jack,' the young fellow said, 'you didn't tell me you were having a breakfast party down here.'

Jack had risen quickly, dropping his napkin in his haste to move over towards the couple, saying, 'Sir William, allow me to introduce my aunt, Lady Bridget, my brother, Nicholas, and his fiancée, Julianne Appleby.'

'Julianne!' the young lady shrieked delightedly and skipped over to join her, 'I didn't expect to find you here!'

Julianne was just as surprised to meet her old school friend, Lucy.

'You must meet my husband, William,' Lucy said proudly. Then added in a whisper, 'we were only married a few days ago.'

'Newly weds!' said Jack triumphantly.

The young couple looked at each other abashed, and bowed.

'We won't interrupt your family breakfast,' Sir William said, 'Come, Lucy my dear, I'm sure the butler will bring us coffee in the morning room.' Holding hands, they disappeared out of the door as quickly as they'd come.

Jack explained, 'They are paying guests here.' Then, turning to Nicholas, he said, 'We have others. I run this house as a honeymoon hotel. But your rooms are always kept free for you — should you find the need to make use of them at any time.'

Julianne was amused to see Nicholas try to hide his anger by picking up his cup to take a gulp of his coffee. She realised that he'd obviously come from the country that morning and had arrived unaware of how his house was being used by his younger brother.

It certainly explained the décor in the house and now she understood that the house was being used as a honeymoon hotel and that the news had somehow

leaked out and was now being discussed and disapproved of by the ton
gossips of Society.

So, that was why Nicholas had been
attempting to dismiss the decorations as
modern art. It explained his discomfi-
ture and feeble excuses. Julianne looked
on with amusement as she noticed
Nicholas's fists open and close as if he
would like to give Jack a good
thrashing.

But the Earl of Featherstonhaugh was
a polished and mature man, certainly
no tongue-tied youth, so he managed to
force a smile and ask, 'Would anyone
care for another cup of coffee?'

Jack seemed at a loss to know how to
deal with his angry older brother.

Yes, thought Julianne, *I like both
brothers, but I can well appreciate how
Nicholas is feeling let down by Jack and
is trying to smooth over this embarrassing situation.*

Then she remembered, Nicholas was
not the only one who had something to
hide.

She was acutely aware that he had, to her great embarrassment, discovered she was not wearing, his ring, surely the most precious possession a fiancée had and would never take it off her hand. How was she going to overcome that? But it was true that she'd mislaid it.

The party sat in a painful silence for a long minute. Even Lady Bridget seemed at a loss to know how to start the conversation again.

'Well now, Jack,' said her ladyship, at last breaking into everyone's thoughts, 'I want you to show me what other alterations you have made to this house, for I am sure now that it is you, and not your brother, who has introduced such wild tastes. And most will need weeding out without delay if my Goddaughter is to live in it.'

Jack had the audacity to laugh and, standing, he went over and drew back his aunt's chair so that she could rise, saying, 'With pleasure, Aunt. Although I can't show you all the rooms upstairs rooms at present . . . I'm sure you understand . . . '

Lady Bridget's steely eyes glared at her nephew as her lips squeezed together. 'No, I don't suppose you can,' she said dryly.

Before she left she looked at Nicholas, saying, 'Now, I want you to give all your attention to Julianne while I'm gone. I'll be off to do some shopping when I've had a tour of the house. I expect to be away at least a couple of hours but I'm sure you will find some thing to amuse her.'

Julianne noticed the Earl's smile. 'Can't I go shopping with you?' she asked, panic rising within her, making her want to follow Lady Bridget, but the lady put up her hand.

'Not today, my dear. You have already brought with you enough gowns and fripperies to fill a shop. Stay here with your fiancé. After you've been apart for so long while he has been in the country, you need to renew your acquaintance with each other.'

'But I need — '

'No buts my dear. Jack shall accompany me to Bond Street to carry my packages for me.'

Why was she pleading to go? Hadn't she come to see Nicholas? To find out if he still really loved her? Now that Lady Bridget had given her that, opportunity she must pull herself together and take the bull by the horns.

But she did feel shaky being left with the Earl. He was bound to question her about his ring.

Nicholas lost no time when they were alone. He slid into the chair next to Julianne and eased it so close to hers their knees touched. Her heart pattered to be so near, and left alone with, the man she loved — yet felt so apprehensive about.

He cleared his throat and said in his tantalisingly attractive voice, 'Are we to sit here just looking at each other in silence for two hours or do you wish to continue where we left off?'

'I don't know what you mean,' she said primly, but her heart pounded.

'Oh, I think you do,' he replied smoothly, cupping her hand with his large bear-like hand and squeezing it gently.

'That was all some time ago now,' she said guardedly.

'I can't think that matters.'

'Mama thinks it does.'

He ran his fingers tenderly around the side of her rosy face saying, 'Do you have to have your mother's permission for everything you do?'

'Of course not!'

He smiled wickedly. 'Then shall we, as my aunt put it, renew our acquaintanceship?'

'Mama thinks we should not.'

He sighed and lifted her chin with one long finger making her startled eyes look directly at him. 'So your mama does rule your life.'

'She tries to, I confess, and as an unmarried lady I am obliged to obey her, at least in most things.'

'She doesn't want you to throw your fortune away on a penniless Earl and a couple of rascally brothers who run a honeymoon hotel, eh?'

Julianne swallowed. That was true, of course, but it was she who was considering getting married, not her mama.

She spoke from her heart, 'I have already decided who I want to marry. And I have a ring to show I am engaged — ' She gave a little gasp at her error in mentioning the ring.

'I think, my dear, you are sometimes a little short on telling the truth.'

Casting her eyes down at her hands, Julianne was nevertheless indignantly defensive when she said, 'I am truthful.'

He was waiting for her to confess she had sent the ring back to him but she did not, so he asked, 'Does it surprise you to know that I still love you, my sweet Julianne?'

'Yes, I am surprised, actually!' she said, making him start. 'After all your initially loving letters you suddenly stopped and sent me no more. What am I supposed to think?'

'But I thought it was you, Julianne, who ceased to pick up your quill and remind me of your undying love?'

'No, it was not. You stopped writing first. You left me wondering if your love for me had ceased.'

He frowned. 'Then I must show you I do love you.' His hooded eyes looked deeply into hers as his lips came to meet hers. Before she knew it he had lifted her to sit on his lap, put his arms around her and kissed her.

The excitement his kisses gave her made Julianne want more. Soft touches that teased her made her slip her hand around his neck to bring him closer, demanding a longer kiss. Thrilled, she drifted into a lingering and passionate embrace.

'Now do you believe I still love you, Julianne?'

'Mmm . . . yes, indeed I do.' But, as Julianne's desire for him increased, so did her sense of decorum. 'But someone may come in,' she whispered in his ear, remembering they were in the dining room with a table of breakfast dishes that the maids would be collecting very soon — and here she was, sitting on his lap!

'I don't suppose the servants here will give a damn, even if they do see us locked together like this.'

She eased herself away from his broad chest and retorted, 'We are most certainly not locked together!'

'Well, no, I suppose we have some way to go yet.'

She was shocked by his candour, yet she wanted to remain where she was, loving the comfort of being in his arms. But she couldn't allow him to think she was entirely committed to him yet while there were still disagreements between them.

She wished there were not as she said, 'I suppose you find me an inexperienced girl. I believe you were — are, by reputation — a rake, my lord.'

'That was true. But now I am reformed.'

She looked around the room at the

art work. 'Not that I can see.'

'Appearances don't count.'

'Oh, yes they do!'

'Then,' he said in all seriousness, 'Why did you take off my ring?'

Julianne slid off his lap and faced him, 'Because Mama said I had to.'

'You told me you don't always obey your mother.'

Exasperated, she replied, 'Well, I didn't want to but Mama kept telling me our engagement was over and that I should remove your ring.'

'What made her say that?'

'Why? Because she'd heard about your Follies Hotel, I expect.'

'It is not my hotel, as well you know.'

Julianne raised her voice, 'But this is your house and this is the Follies Hotel. You can't blame my mother for putting two and two together.'

'All this is Jack's fault.'

'And partly yours too.'

'How can it be my fault?'

'It was unwise of you to give your house to Jack to look after. You can't blame him entirely for designing this disreputable money-making palace.'

Nicholas scowled at her.

'And you've put me in a dilemma,' she went on, 'I have to decide if I want to be associated with . . . with a Follies Hotel.'

He stood, looming over her, 'What has this Follies Hotel do with us? How can you think it is over between us? After the way you've just kissed me, I doubt very much that is how you truly feel.'

Flushing, Julianne stuttered but could think of nothing to say.

'Do you seriously think I would jilt you?'

She looked up into his angry eyes. 'I wondered . . . '

He turned and stamped around the room like a bear pacing his cage. 'Julianne,' he thundered in a pained voice, 'how could you even consider I would ever want any other woman but you?'

'Easily,' she snapped back. She felt cross.

'After my promise to marry you? Do

you really think I would abandon you?' he asked her incredulously.

'Certainly. That what rakes do, isn't it? Take one lover after another.'

'Youthful follies have nothing to do with true love!'

Julianne was pleased to see she'd rattled him. 'Love? Just look at this house full of follies,' she cried. 'Is this sort of romantic artwork supposed to woo me? Because it does not.'

'I did not intend for you to see this décor.'

'Oh? All this,' she waved her hand around the room, 'was intended for your other ladies, is that it?'

'No, damn it!'

'Then who is it for?'

'You know perfectly well it has nothing to do with me. It is all my brother's idea. I gave him the house to look after while I was wrestling with my inherited estate finances and he has — without my knowledge, as you full well know — turned my house into a . . . a . . . '

'A brothel?'

'You shouldn't know that word!'

'You shouldn't tell me what I should or should not know, Nicholas. Just look at what you have allowed here! The romantic content is grossly overstated and really quite base! And earlier you were acting as though you either did not notice, or . . . or . . . '

He chortled.

'Or,' she continued, 'you are actually amused by it!'

A loud groan escaped his lips. 'How many times do I have to explain to you what happened? I had nothing to do with this recent altered décor in my house. Jack did it all. He has informed us that it as been designed as a honeymoon hotel — for married couples.'

'I'm sure Jack vets most carefully anyone who wants to stay here — even for a few hours. It's a money-making venture and I make no excuse for our family's need to do that. But now it will go.'

'Oh?' She sat down heavily on a nearby chair and traced her finger around an eyebrow as she pondered.

She had to agree the idea of a place where newly married couples could come and make love in complete privacy and with complete respectability, was a good idea. She knew it could be very difficult for lovers sometimes, especially for people wanting to keep to Society's conventions yet at the same time to indulge in their passion for each other.

A small pang of sorrow for Jack hit her and she enquired, 'What will happen to Jack's hotel?'

'It is to be moved as soon as I have the opportunity to organise it. I'll want my wife to decorate my houses as she wishes. Jack should certainly not have turned the place into a . . . a frightful, commercial venture. I came to London post haste when I learned about it, only you arrived before I could start removing both him and his follies. There, that is the simple truth of it.'

'Well you may dismiss it as you please. But I can't see that the rumours going round about you and the Follies Hotel will cease, even when the house is brought back to normal.'

Julianne was alarmed when he didn't reply. He'd turned his back on her.

'Of course,' she said in a low conciliatory voice, 'I shouldn't be blaming you for the troubles other people have inflicted upon you . . . '

He still didn't say anything. Had she overstepped the mark?

Worried now that she might have insulted him and thereby possibly lost his esteem by her self-righteous condemnation of his brother's actions and his lack of funds, she said, 'No, it shouldn't make any difference to us. I'm sorry. It was unfair of me to blame you, Nicholas.'

He was breathing heavily. 'I must admit,' he said cautiously, 'I should have kept a better eye on Jack, for I know that he, like the Prince Regent himself, overdoes everything, showing a lack of prudence. Jack has only used his wits to provide what he thought was a needed convenience for honeymooners. And, for what it is, I think he's made a pretty good job of it.' Nicholas's expression gradually warmed into a smile, as he chuckled. 'And since it's supposed to be a lover's paradise, maybe we should take advantage of that?'

Pinker in the face than she wished to be, Julianne stood in a quandary. Should she make for the door? She copied her mother's haughty voice, 'My lord, I don't think you understand how unpleasant this visit to your house has been for me, seeing all this blatantly erotic art.'

'Unpleasant for you!' Nicholas bellowed indignantly at her disapproving manner. 'How do you think it's been for me, with my dear aunt clearly showing her disapproval?'

Julianne looked up into his eyes. 'To be fair, I would say we have both been somewhat surprised as well as scandalised.'

He laughed a little. 'Well, my sweet, if that is all you feel it is, we should dismiss it all just as if we had suffered having to eat a bad dinner, by accepting the unsavoury art works round here for what they are — unnecessary romantic stimulus needed by some. But not by us for you and I both know we'll make love when we want one another.' Then he added with a mischievous twinkle in his eyes, 'Right now, if you like?'

'Nicholas! You are outrageous!'

'Julianne Appleby. Where has your sense of humour gone? You're behaving like your mother,' he said with a disappointed tone.

Julianne shrank inside, realising he had a point. She was being overly straight-laced and she wasn't nearly as upset about the Follies Hotel as she'd suggested she was. In fact, she was secretly just as amused by it all as he seemed to be.

He went on, 'I always thought you were a fun-loving girl who enjoyed me making love to you. Either you wish to marry me or you do not. So, make up your mind — what would you like to do?'

The chiming on the mantle shelf clock made Julianne's hot face turn towards it to note that the time was getting on and her Godmother would be back before long.

And she was not any nearer to feeling that the misunderstandings between them had been cleared up. Certainly he had not told her why he had stopped writing to her, nor why he did not seem to believe her when she said that she had lost his ring.

But she didn't want to lose him either; in fact, the more she was with him, the more she wanted him very much. But how could she shake the truth out of him? 'I'd like to go out and walk in the garden,' she said with a challenging smile.

★　★　★

Julianne liked gardens and she genuinely enjoyed seeing the spring flowers in his town house garden. Gardens were restful, and she felt they both needed the respite from the tussle they were in.

Nicholas seemed pleased to be able to break away from the redecorated interior he'd told her he disliked. He seemed to relax as they crunched over the gravel paths, smelling the fragrant box hedging and stopping to sniff the sweet clusters from the lilac bush. It was pleasant to walk with him, Julianne thought, just to enjoy his company with no arguments.

'Have you been able to sort out the financial affairs of the estate your father left you?' she asked.

'I'm debt free now, but still low in pocket until the estates start making a good profit again. But I expect that they will very soon.'

'Forgive me, Nicholas, I didn't mean to pry.'

'You have the right to know. You must realise I may not at first be able to provide you with the very high standard of living you are used to.'

Julianne stopped to admire some primroses. 'Look, at those primroses, Nicholas. They are my favourite flowers. Although they are not the most showy blooms in the garden, I like their colour and simplicity.'

'I like them too.'

She looked up into his eyes, saying, 'I like simple living. I don't need or want to have luxury. Yes, I enjoy nice clothes and a pleasant house to live in but I don't like opulence.

'I'm sure I'd be able to decorate a house with elegance and style using little money. Anyway, you already own a fine town house, and a country seat you tell me you love, and I'm sure I will love it too. They will just need straightforward maintenance, that's all.

'What you are able to provide would give everything we need for us.' And for our family, she thought to herself.

'What about your fortune?'

She giggled. 'Well, that may come in useful at times!'

He laughed too, then with all

seriousness said, 'Your money is not why I want to marry you, Julianne.'

'I know that. Money doesn't bring happiness, Nicholas. My Mama is wealthy, but it hasn't given her any more than a life of luxury with nothing worthwhile to do with herself — except to scheme and try climbing higher on the social ladder.'

Nicholas kicked a stone along the path. 'And what is it that you want to do with your life?'

'Travel the world.'

'It's a big place.'

Julianne thought for a moment, then with her eyes sparkling in anticipation, she said, 'We could go to Paris. I'd love to see Paris — and Vienna. But I expect you did the grand tour when you came of age?'

Nicholas breathed deeply. 'I went to university. Then Papa died. I have yet to make a grand tour of Europe.'

'Do you want to?'

Nicholas laughed. 'With you, yes.'

Naturally Julianne felt she would prefer to go abroad with Nicholas. It would be much more fun than going as a single woman, even though she was an heiress, and could take all the servants she needed with her.

But Julianne didn't say that she would like to go travelling with him, although she ached to tell him she loved him and wanted him with her for the rest of her life.

Unfortunately, she felt frustrated because she wanted him to make the first move to make their relationship perfect. She needed him to explain why he'd given up writing to her, and she wanted him to cease giving her the impression he didn't believe her when she said she had lost his ring.

They walked on a little way without talking.

Meeting a gardener who was weeding the vegetable plot they stopped and Nicholas discussed the weather and plans the gardener had for the coming seeding and cultivation.

Meanwhile Julianne's mind was wondering what she could do to break the impasse. She couldn't do anything about finding the ring, especially as she was now in London and the ring had been lost at her home.

She wondered about the letters. Nicholas had told her he had continued to write to her long after she'd stopped writing to him. Surely he was speaking the truth? So what happened to those letters he said he wrote to her that she had never received?

She was touched when he plucked a sweet smelling lilac blossom and handed it to her. He was a thoughtful man. So what could she do to convince him that she still seriously wanted to marry him? Even when he'd asked her bluntly if she still wanted to marry him, she hadn't given him an equally straight answer, which wasn't very nice of her.

But maybe it was a good idea to let him think she was not easy to get. She must make him realise that if he wanted her, he must trust her — and be honest with her.

She must convince him that she was being honest and, regretfully, had truly lost his ring.

So far, she felt they had both admitted that they still loved one another — passionately — so what did the missing ring matter, any more than her wealth? They needed neither.

All they needed was more time to sort out the painful misunderstandings that had arisen between them.

It was getting near the time Aunt Bridget would be returning and would want her lunch. Julianne suggested they went in to wait for her.

When Aunt Bridget came home from her shopping trip, she looked carefully at Julianne, and then at Nicholas. She pursed her lips and shook her head as she observed that nothing had really been fully resolved between the two of them.

But Aunt Bridget had a full pro-gramme of events in mind for them both to attend in the next few weeks.

'And you will please make yourself

available to escort Julianne to every one of them,' she told Nicholas.

'Yes, indeed Aunt,' he answered with a bow, 'If it is Julianne's wish?'

'It certainly is,' Julianne smiled her agreement.

She was determined to have as much time with him as possible. She was just as proud of Nicholas as she ever was. And was delighted he'd said he would be able to escort her during the season's activities.

They would show those gossips that their prattling about the Follies Hotel — something that *they* themselves had turned into scandal — was not harming the Earl of Featherstonehaugh, or his future countess, which she hoped she would soon be.

And when Jack said he would like to join the party on their outings, she was pleased about that too. Jack would be so much fun to have around.

Nicholas barked at his young brother, 'Before you do anything, you are to hire some carters and get them to remove all of your artifacts from my house. And find the original pictures you took down from the walls and put them back where they belong.'

Jack grinned. 'I will, with pleasure! For you see, dear brother, I have been fortunate enough to have made enough money already to buy another house for my Follies Hotel,' he said proudly.

'As long as I have nothing to do with it,' Nicholas said, 'I wish you well.'

'Well done, Jack,' Julianne said, and Jack smiled back at her warmly.

'Perhaps you'd be so gracious as to help me decorate my new hotel, dearest Julianne?' he asked her. Much to Nicholas's annoyance, she said she'd love to, although she said she may not agree with all the art work he might want to put in it.

She received a scowl from her fiancée but, as it was her intention to make Nicholas realise she wasn't going to let him think he could take her for granted and admit to things she hadn't done, she ignored it.

Perhaps if she flirted a little during the season, it would make Nicholas jealous and help to shake the truth out of him?

5

An exciting time began for Julianne, with the London Season in full swing. She had been though it all before, so she suffered none of the nerves about her looks or behaviour that most young ladies straight out of the schoolroom did. Nor had she to hunt for a suitable husband, which was the purpose of the Season for most young women, because she already had one: she was engaged.

And so it appeared was Nicholas, because he hadn't ended their engagement and continued to act, as she did, as if they were still betrothed. However, he appeared clearly irked as time went on that she wouldn't admit to sending back his ring. And she kept repeating that she didn't know what had happened to the ring he'd given her — and demanding he owned up to stopping writing to her before she did.

Nicholas turned up with his brother, Jack, to escort the ladies to every function. Aunt Bridget was gratified they did as Nicholas and Julianne attended assemblies, balls, card parties, musical evenings and theatre visits, where they were seen in public — and, she was well aware of it, whispered about everywhere they went.

Swirling around as she danced with Nicholas one evening he asked her, 'Doesn't it bother you, my sweet, that we are the talk of the ton?'

Julianne waited until the musical steps brought them closer together and replied, 'What are they saying?'

'That you are not wearing my engagement ring.'

'Gracious me. Have they nothing better to talk about? Perhaps I should send them to find it.'

Nicholas chuckled. 'That is not the only reason we are news. Someone has told them we are no longer engaged — so they are intrigued to see us dancing together as though we still love one another.'

'Who would spread a rumour like that?'

'I have my suspicions who it might be . . .'

'Who? Not Jack, I hope?'

Nicholas shook his head as he took her hand and kissed it before escorting her down the line of dancers in time to the music. 'My brother would not dare rob me of my beautiful lady.'

Julianne glanced around at the other gentlemen dancers and noted their paunches, their bald heads and chinless faces, and decided no one in the ton would dare either. Nicholas stood out like a splendid god; tall and looking more handsome than ever in evening dress, Nicholas was also a natural dancer who was treating her with every courtesy.

She smiled to have the best man in the room as a partner. But then she frowned asking, 'Why should anyone want to spit us up?'

'Perhaps because they have been told that I'm the owner of the Follies Hotel and they think it's a disgrace.'

Julianne stopped dancing and stamped her foot. 'But you are not!'

He took her hand and urged her to continue dancing, 'We know that. So we shall ignore how some look at us and what they say about the Follies Hotel — but we cannot ignore that it has come between us.'

Julianne continued with her dance steps regretting she had to agree. 'Will we ever be able to live it down?'

'Only if we marry.'

Julianne felt tears come into her eyes. She desperately wanted to marry him. He attracted her like a butterfly to a flower. Even the scent of him she liked. Indeed she'd been praying every night that their search for what really happened to her ring and the letters would soon be over.

But it seemed as though the Season would end and nothing would be settled between them.

Something had to be done — and fast.

Julianne wondered if she should be

spending more time with other eligible men and so make Nicholas begin to wonder if she was becoming less attracted to him.

That evening she confided in Lady Bridget, saying that she felt she must consider other men to marry because Nicholas was simply expecting too much from her.

'How can I admit to something he thinks I've done when I haven't?' she wailed. 'I must either make him believe me or find another man to marry.'

Lady Bridget declared, 'No, no, Julianne. You must understand that a man in love is single-minded, very single-minded indeed, and needs his chosen bride to be so, too.'

Julianne was tired after the ball and fell back into the cushions of the sofa in an unlady-like manner her mama would have objected to. 'I'm at my wits end. What shall I do?'

Her ladyship sat upright and took a sip of her evening posset. 'You love Nicholas, don't you?'

'With all my heart.'

Her ladyship's eyes were fixed hard on the tired girl. 'And you do want to marry him?'

'There is no doubt in my mind. The more we are together the more I feel I want him. And I believe he feels the same way about me.'

'Then you must show him that it is so.'

'I dare not go further than I do or he would have me in bed in a trice!'

Taking too quick a sip of her posset, the regal lady coughed, then said, 'Indeed! That will not solve anything. I shall see what I can do.'

★   ★   ★

So Aunt Bridget made a point of speaking to her nephew privately one afternoon when Julianne was out shopping and assisting Jack in choosing some furnishings for his new hotel.

She summoned Nicholas to come to see her.

He found his aunt in her elegant drawing room waiting for him with a silver tea kettle and stand on the table, ready for her maid to make them afternoon refreshment.

After going up to his aunt and kissing her on the cheek, Nicholas sat down on the strongest looking chair he could see; most of his aunt's chairs looked fashionable but spindly to him.

After the maid had made the tea she handed the lady and gentleman cups of the beverage, bobbed a curtsy and left the room.

'Well now, Aunt. What can I do you for you?' he asked pleasantly, hiding his own deep apprehension.

She patted her new and highly fashionable Turkish style headdress. 'Now, Nicholas, I am going to be completely honest with you,' she began.

'Aunt Bridget, I wouldn't expect you be otherwise.'

She cleared her throat. 'As you know, it is not my way to interfere with other's people's business.'

Nicholas thought just the opposite — she was very skilled at it — but knowing she was a good woman at heart he made no comment.

She went on, 'I have to tell you that you have been looking decidedly miserable ever since you came to London. And I think I know why.'

Nicholas picked up his teacup and drank thirstily.

She raised her voice saying, 'You are not making enough effort to win back Julianne,' she told him sharply.

Nicholas almost tipped his teacup over as he jerked his hand when putting it down on the small table beside him. 'My dear aunt, how can you say that?' He sounded most aggrieved. 'I've remained in London to escort you and Julianne for weeks now, when I really need to get back to Featherstone Hall to resume making sure that everyone there is keeping up to scratch. The harvest will be due for reaping soon.'

Aunt Bridget's steely eyes were rivetted on his. 'Forget the harvest.

There are enough good workers on your estates to take care of it. You need to think of your heir.'

Jack sat up and straightened his cravat. 'What do you mean?'

'You know perfectly well what I mean. You need a son and heir, unless you want Jack, or some distant cousin to inherit? I think not. But first you need to marry. The season will be ending soon and you still have made no progress in pacifying Julianne, who would make you an excellent wife.'

'That is hardly my fault, Aunt. I fear my beautiful fiancée is stubborn, insisting I stopped writing to her before she stopped writing to me.'

'Julianne is a strong minded young lady and that's a good thing. In fact, having a mother like she has, it is not surprising to me that she can be a touch deceitful at times — I wouldn't trust that mother of hers an inch!'

'I'm not intending to marry Mrs Appleby, Aunt. It's her daughter's character that concerns me.'

Lady Bridget gave a long sigh. 'Fortunately Julianne takes after her dear father. He was an honest gentleman.'

'We are discussing my beloved, not her ancestors.'

'Then concentrate on Julianne yourself, Nicholas. She is a jewel you are allowing to slip out of your grasp.'

Nicholas gulped the rest of his tea quickly and crashed his cup and saucer down on the little table. The cup wobbled dramatically and had to steady it with his big hand. 'I repeat. Julianne is not altogether truthful. She won't tell me why she isn't wearing my engagement ring. She's been inventing all kinds of excuses for it.'

'But you know perfectly well why that is, Nicholas. The poor gel is simply embarrassed that she's lost it. She can't help that. Get her another one.'

Nicholas sighed. 'I can't afford to keep her in engagement rings. The one I bought her used up the last of my cash before I started to pay off father's debts. The one I gave her was — is — a lovely ring.' He felt in his pocket for it and fingered it. 'Julianne told me she said she liked it when I gave it to her and said she would never take it off.'

'Well, she did take it off. She told me her mama insisted your engagement was over. But she came to London because she didn't think it was. So why can't you settle it between you?'

'I have asked her if she still loves me — she didn't give me an answer. Although, most of the time she is acting as though she does. In fact I'm certain she does.'

Now it was Aunt Bridget's turn to take in a long breath and let it out slowly. 'Of course she does! That's precisely why I have asked you here today. You've antagonised her. And you're not making enough effort to heal the wound and woo her again. After all she is an heiress and I've noticed plenty of young men are after her — '

'So have I,' he said icily. 'Surely you

know she's playing a game with me? Deliberately provoking me because she wants me to admit that I stopped writing to her first, when I did not.'

'What does it matter who stopped writing first? Or what happened to your ring? It'll turn up before long, like lost keys they are found eventually. What a pair of quarrelsome children you are being, attaching so much importance to trifles!'

Nicholas reddened, almost feeling the ring burning in his pocket. 'So you may think. But I put a lot of importance on trust and honesty. I want to start our married life knowing we can rely on one another. I don't want mysterious goings on between us.'

'I don't know about starting your romance — it sounds to me as if you have already ended it!'

Nicholas clenched his fists. 'No, it is not ended. I don't intend to lose Julianne and I'm sure she still wants me, otherwise she would have dashed off with some other fellow by now.'

'Well, heaven knows how this bumble-broth will end. I can't keep bringing Julianne to London Season after Season. She'll become an old maid before it's settled between the two of you.'

Nicholas gave a sudden chuckle. 'She'll give in before long. You'll see.'

'No! I don't see that at all. Julianne Appleby is a very determined young lady. I think it will be you coming to me in tears because you've lost her to another suitor — and she has plenty of them.'

'They are after her fortune.'

'As are you.'

Nicholas shook his head. 'No, Aunt, I'm not. It would come in useful, I grant you that, but I can manage without her money and I have told her so.'

'I'm sure she was most impressed.'

Nicholas shook his head. 'How do I know what she thinks? I only know I love Julianne. We are well suited and I want to marry her. And I believe — although she won't say so at present

— that she wants to marry me. So all I can do is to wait until she gives in and tells me the truth.'

He said this with a sudden pang of shame at his own subterfuge, knowing perfectly well she wouldn't be able to find her ring while he had it.

'Oh, dear, oh, dear! That is exactly what she has told me about you. I think you will never win her back that way. Women don't like to give in. They need to be enticed.'

Nicholas, hearing tinkling chimes, looked at the ornate clock on the mantelshelf. 'She'll be back here soon. I'd better be off.'

'You're running away?'

'No, I just don't want to hear about what she and Jack have purchased for his new Follies Hotel. She should be buying new things for our house.'

Aunt Bridget looked at his retreating figure but before he'd crossed the large room and reached the door she called after him, 'Nicholas, all this Season you have been a perfect escort but your behaviour hasn't quietened the ton gibble-gabblers. They are watching you and Julianne as if you were actors on a stage. They are rejoicing in your theatrical performance but I am not. You must bring this farce to an end.'

He turned round to her look at his aunt, sitting there like a judge, and said, 'I suggest you tell Julianne that.'

'She knows what I think. She has been in tears about it.'

He frowned. 'Tears? Julianne? I thought she was a strong woman.'

'Yes, indeed she is. But you don't seem to realise how unkind you are being to her. Trying to make her admit to something she knows nothing about. Or perhaps she doesn't want to admit she took the ring off in a fit of anger when you stopped writing to her. And then she forgot where she put it. She may have been cross enough to have thrown it in a pond or river, and she doesn't like to admit it. You have to allow women some leeway.'

Nicholas hadn't thought of that. He

was only sure Julianne was being deliberately annoying to him by flirting with other men. 'I don't want to hurt her,' he said flatly. 'I'll have to think of a way to stop this unhappiness.'

'Then I beg you to retreat from your warfare with her. Girls like to be made to feel admired and loved and to feel secure enough to be able to love in return. That's all you need do — show her you truly love her. When did you last hold her in your arms and kiss her?'

Nicholas pursed his lips. His aunt was definitely taking Julianne's side in this argument. But perhaps he was wrong to have demanded that Julianne told him what had happened to his ring — especially as he had it.

Yes, perhaps he shouldn't expect her to admit she went down to the post office with a small packet and returned his ring. It might be too humiliating for her to have to admit that.

Suddenly he decided one way he could get out of this impasse was that he could produce the ring and ask her if she still wanted it.

'My dearest aunt,' Nicholas said, somewhat chastened. 'I love you dearly for the way in which you are trying to help us. I intend to rise above the problem and resolve it once and for all.'

As he left the room he blew her a kiss and she almost shouted at him, 'Send your kisses Julianne's way. She needs them more than I!'

He smiled at her as he closed the door behind him. 'I'll be seeing you both this evening,' he chortled.

But his smile didn't last as he trotted down the front steps of his aunt's house and he began to walk towards Mayfair.

Several high-class ladies and gentleman turned to look at the exquisitely turned out young man who strode purposefully along the pavement. He could almost hear their comments. Isn't that the Earl of Featherstonhaugh, the owner of that shocking Follies Hotel? Fine figure of a man that young Earl, but have you heard the latest rumours about him? It is said he is engaged to the young heiress, Miss Julianne Appleby, but you rarely see them out together. She frequently dances with other gentlemen and almost seems to ignore him.

Nicholas ran his cane along some iron railings in the front of a house as he marched by, making an unholy racket which drew attention to himself, as if he hadn't enough unwelcome attention already.

But what did he care what other people said? And yet he knew it did matter to him, for it had spoilt his relationship with Julianne.

It wasn't pleasant to be the subject of the world's speculation. For everyone to look at him askance, seeing his chosen lady looking at other gentlemen and enjoying their company instead of his. And as for her decision not to wear his engagement ring, Julianne had succeeded in making him look an oddity.

He was sure someone had been fanning the flames of gossip that had been so harmful to his beloved and himself. And thinking about what his aunt had just said, he now realised who that tittle-tattler might be.

Aunt Bridget was right. This ridiculous charade must end.

The only good he could think of about the position he was in was that he knew he loved Julianne and he was sure she loved him, although their love was being severely tested.

He just needed the opportunity to show her, and everyone in Society, that he had left his rakish days behind him and had become a responsible member of the aristocracy and would make a worthy husband and father.

By this time his polished boots had pounded all the way to Mayfair and he'd reached his town house and skipped up the steps leading to the front door. Having given his hat and cane to Biggs his butler, he felt elated to think that all his woes and worries might actually soon be over.

He began eating his lunch with relish, looking forward to the evening's ball and to seeing Julianne, because he'd decided he would swallow his pride and have her forever in his arms.

Of course she may not like it when he offered her his ring again, explaining that he'd had it for some time, as he planned to do. But he wouldn't demand an explanation of who had sent it to him. All he wanted was that they become true lovers.

He held his wine glass at eye level and swirled the contents around before he drank from it. He knew his happiness and Julianne's depended on his dealings with her this evening.

He'd never wanted anything so much as that this night should see an end to their estrangement.

He raised his glass, said, 'Here's to you, my beautiful Julianne. May our love overcome our differences tonight.'

6

That night at the Duke and Duchess of Chubb's grand ball, Julianne was wearing her prettiest gown and her hair was dressed by the best hairdresser in town. Miss Appleby was a young lady who turned men's heads to admire her. Being naturally attractive, it had been easy for her to flirt a little during that evening as she had planned, despite Lady Bridget's advice not to. She still wanted to ensure that Nicholas would think that she was by no means his until he admitted he had stopped writing to her during the winter and explained why he had. She considered he still had to convince her that her love for him could not simply be taken for granted.

But as the evening progressed, she soon noted Nicholas's disapproval as she gave dances to other partners. Soon she began to wish she'd had more sense than to try and attract other men, because once she'd shown that she was not exclusively attached to Nicholas any more and was available to enjoy other young men's company, they never left her alone.

So, although she'd accomplished what she'd intended, it had not made her happy. Comparing the many young men she became surrounded by with Nicholas only made her feel sure she'd chosen the right man to marry.

Unfortunately, just as she wanted to return to being his adoring fiancée, she became aware that Nicholas had made himself scarce. While she was enjoying the company of other people, he'd left her to talk to his friends, to drink a bottle of wine with them and play cards.

She began to miss him being there beside her. It was embarrassing to find he was not there to ask her to dance.

He'd left her to Jack's tender care — and Jack's friends were not the kind of young men who interested her. Just the opposite, in fact, as she began to dislike one or two of them as silly, fashionable dandies, who only thought about their looks, giggled like girls, and danced abominably.

Of course, this pantomime had not gone unnoticed by Society's gossip mongers, who already had enough ammunition against her and Nicholas. It had been foolish of her to allow it to grow. If anything she learned that it was utter folly to play with a good man's affections.

Why should she be surprised when Nicholas turned his back on her? Did he think she might behave like that when she was married to him?

He could break off their engagement — she snapped her fingers — just like that. Looking at her bare left hand she felt tears come to her eyes as she missed seeing his ring on her finger.

How she had loved that ring that had symbolised their love.

What could have happened to it? She'd asked herself that question all day long for months.

Feeling more confident than ever that she loved the right man, she longed for him to take her in his arms and kiss her and to know they were close friends again.

So now Julianne had the problem of convincing Nicholas that she loved him and that she would say yes, immediately, if he asked her to marry him again — as he had done right at the beginning of the Season when she had unwisely rebuffed him.

Earlier in the day when Nicholas had visited his Aunt Bridget, Julianne had been out shopping with Jack. He still needed to make some decisions about the wallpaper he wanted for his new hotel. She found this exercise very trying because Jack had extraordinary tastes and she had the greatest difficulty in persuading him that if he must have furnishing that would be exotic and different then he would be better to go for the Chinese style the Prince of Wales was known to have favoured at the Royal Pavilion.

As Julianne drew his attention away from some very unsuitable wallpaper to some delicately coloured paper with exquisitely drawn trees in blossom with birds fluttering about, she noticed her newly-wed school friend, Lucy, now young Lady Dunning, in the shop.

'Why, Julianne, how lovely to see you again,' her friend, Lucy, declared. 'I've only seen you from afar on the dance floor at several parties. But where is your fiancé? You never seem to be together.'

Julianne, taken off guard, replied, 'Goodness me, I don't know. He must be somewhere around. I'm out shopping with his brother, Jack, and I'd better go and find him. Goodbye.'

★ ★ ★

But Julianne wasn't spared from Lucy's attention for long because that evening, when she'd been dancing with other men, they met again at the Duke and

Duchess of Chubb's ball.

Over the dance music and the clatter of the men's shoes on the wooden dance floor, Lucy looked at her and whispered, 'You look lovely in that stylish muslin gown, Julianne — I wish I had your figure. But I'm sure you've noticed there's a great deal of gossip around the ton about you and the Earl of Featherstonhaugh.'

Julianne tried to look disdainfully indifferent. 'Oh, yes? I can't think what that could be about.'

Lucy reminded her. 'There is prattle amongst the ladies that the Earl is the real owner of the Follies Hotel and that you have sent his ring back.'

Julianne swallowed hard and smiled a little self-consciously, then she tossed her head so violently a flower flew out of her headdress and landed on to the floor. 'I'm well aware of that chit-chat, Lucy, but I believe they are just jealous of the handsome man I have captured to marry.'

But Lucy was persistent. 'I know it

was his house in Mayfair where William and I spent our honeymoon. You were there too, remember?'

Julianne was stunned. Never before had she thought what a nuisance it would be to have rumours spread about. Her mother had been right when she'd said scandal shredded reputations.

'No,' Julianne replied sharply, 'Nicholas is not the owner of the Follies Hotel, his brother is. And the business has now been moved from Nicholas's house in any case.'

'That's why I was shopping for wallpaper with Jack when you saw me earlier today. He needs someone sensible to guide his choice of furnishings. The last time when he decorated Nicholas's house it was quite shocking, even though he had tried to base it upon classical art forms.'

Lucy gave an embarrassed giggle. 'It was a bit, wasn't it?' she said.

'You were madly in love at the time, Lucy. You only had eyes for your beloved William. I'm sure you wouldn't now choose to stay at a hotel with such outlandish furnishings.'

Lucy had the grace to colour. 'Now I come to think on it, some of the pictures were a little . . . '

'Indeed,' Julianne nodded. 'They were not to my taste either. So I'm now trying to guide Jack as to what would be considered acceptable. Believe me, Lucy, it isn't easy. Even though Jack is a dear chap, he has about as much sense as a parrot.'

'Lord Milverton? A parrot?'

'Well,' said Julianne, 'he is a likable young man but he likes to look gaudy. Just look over there at the way he's dressed tonight. His bright orange jacket wouldn't be out of place in a jungle and his blue striped trousers are far too striking. I'm overlooked when out with him because everyone sniggers and makes comments about his attire!'

Lucy looked over at Jack and hid her smile behind her fan. 'I can see what you mean.'

Julianne went on, 'And Jack does talk a lot of amusing nonsense at times, does he not? But that is not to say I don't like him — and I think parrots are lovely birds!'

Lucy giggled then said confidentially, 'William thinks Jack a bit of a joke, too, and said his hotel deserved to be mocked. The Follies Hotel, once seen will never be forgotten, was what William said about it.'

Horrified that may be so, Julianne began to wonder again if she really wished to become associated with all of this.

But she loved Nicholas and she didn't want to give him up just because he was known as the owner of the Follies Hotel. So she decided she must brazen her way though all the scandalous rumours.

She explained to Lucy, 'Nicholas's house was used only temporarily when he was in the country during the winter months. Jack's hotel has now moved to new premises. Anyway, as I told you, his brother, Jack, the Viscount Milverton, is the owner of the Follies Hotel. And you would do me and Nicholas a kindness to tell everyone that and scotch the rumour that the Follies Hotel is Nicholas's brainwave.'

Lucy examined her friend. 'I'll certainly try, for your sake, but I think I'll have trouble persuading everyone that Nicholas is not the owner. He's already known to be a rake — '

'I know he was, Lucy, but he's changed now.'

'They say Earl Featherstonhaugh is as poor as a country mouse and that's why he set up the Follies Hotel in his house.'

Julianne was becoming cross, although she did her best to control her temper. 'You mean to tell me that they all think that's the reason why he is marrying me? No, you are wrong about that, quite wrong,' Julianne said firmly. 'Nicholas no longer needs to obtain funds to pay off his father's debts since he has already done that himself, with no help from my fortune. Not a penny of it, Lucy. Indeed, he has set up his estates very well over the winter and they will thrive and give him a good income in the future.'

'Mmm,' Lucy muttered, 'then, he is a good catch for any young lady. But I have noticed, as many have, that you are not wearing his ring.'

Julianne pretended she didn't care that Lucy had noticed her missing ring. But she was devastated to be reminded that other people might have noticed it too.

'Oh, it's at the jewellers being altered,' she said as lightly as she could, hoping her latest lie about the missing ring would not eventually get back to Nicholas. She knew her mother to be deceitful at times and she didn't want to become like her.

'Lucy, listen to me, will you? I'm not unaware of his lordship's faults, as he is aware of mine. I cannot stop wagging tongues but we would not be partaking of the Season's engagements together if we did not want to appear in public as a betrothed couple now, would we?'

'We truly love one another, although we're not rushing into marriage since we have to sort out certain . . . difficulties first.'

What else could she say to Lucy? The missing ring was a private matter between herself and Nicholas.

Just at that moment some good fortune appeared at just the right time, or at least it appeared to be fortunate at the time, though little did Julianne know that it was to turn out to be a most unfortunate thing.

Julianne and Lucy's conversation was interrupted because a gentleman came up to Julianne, bowed, and asked her to dance.

Under normal circumstances, Julianne would have politely refused to take this man's hand but she was so anxious to end her embarrassing conversation and Lucy's intrusive questioning about her private relationship with Nicholas.

The gentleman who led her onto the

dance floor was a man most mamas warned their young daughters to avoid. A fortune hunter by the name of Baron Percy Browne. Where he came from nobody seemed to know or even care. Certainly he would not even have come to Julianne's attention if she had not been flirting earlier in the evening.

Being officially engaged, Julianne had not been supervised as carefully as other young ladies. Aunt Bridget didn't consider it necessary to hold her on a tight rein. Anyway, Aunt Bridget felt she was doing an important job of sitting with the older ladies and quelling the gossip mongers with their tales about the Follies Hotel.

She had also thought that Nicholas was escorting Julianne and that Jack was dancing with her too.

Years of practice enabled Baron Browne to sniff out the women with money whom he needed to impress and although he had not managed to capture an heiress, he always hoped he could track one down.

So that evening, when he discovered Julianne Appleby, whom he had been told had a vast fortune, his piggy eyes glistened at the amount she was said to have inherited.

Pointed out to him, he could see she was not only worth a mint of money, but she was lovely to look at — and appeared to have no chaperone.

But he soon found when he danced with Julianne that she was no silly chit. The Baron realised he would need a proper plan of action if he wanted to secure her as his bride.

However, Lady Bridget was well aware of Baron Browne's reputation and noticed the Baron's snake-like figure encircling her charge. But her ladyship was in a bit of a dilemma. Although she had to protect Julianne from undesirable men — and every chaperone knew that there were several around all the parties that their girls must avoid — she had intended to keep well away from Julianne that evening on purpose.

She wanted Nicholas to have the chance to talk privately to Julianne, because now she hoped she'd convinced Nicholas that he must go down on his bended knee to woo his bride, and that he should do it that very evening. Lady Bridget felt sure that all would then be well between the estranged pair.

But Julianne was being punished for not taking her advice. As the evening wore on, Julianne found that her enthusiasm for dancing and chatting to friends, or even the opportunity of strolling in the well-laid out flower gardens, gave her no enjoyment.

She had no appetite to visit the refreshment rooms for a lemonade, nor to play cards with Jack. She became sick of hearing other men compliment her on her appearance, when she only wanted Nicholas to admire her.

Nor could she tolerate any more disapproving glances from members of the ton when she walked by them. And she loathed overhearing nasty remarks about her fiancé, which were completely untrue.

All she wanted was for Nicholas to come to her and make her evening by being with her. She looked around for his familiar impeccably turned-out figure and wondered where he had got to that evening.

Of course it was all her fault that he was not to be seen. Could she blame him for having to attend functions evening after evening to see her preferring other men's company to his?

The horrid thought struck her that, as she was playing about, he may begin dallying with other ladies. So far she had neither seen nor heard that he was, but could she blame him if he did, after her behaviour?

She sat down feeling tired and discontented, fanning her warm face.

A footman came up and bowed. 'I have a note from the Earl of Featherstonhaugh for Miss Julianne Appleby,' he intoned.

She practically snatched the note he

offered out to her on a silver tray.

'Thank you,' she said, dismissing him with a flick of her gloved hand, so that she could read the missive in private. She opened it to read:

My dearest Julianne,

Please come to the orangery at ten o'clock. I must speak with you.

Your loving Nicholas.

Julianne smiled and looked around anxiously to find a clock and because she didn't see one, she decided to go to Aunt Bridget and ask her what the time was and to tell her that she would be meeting Nicholas in the orangery.

In her haste she didn't notice that the note Nicholas had sent her slipped to the floor.

But Baron Browne did.

When Julianne tripped off to see her Godmother to tell her that she was meeting Nicholas, hoping it would be a chance for them to talk in private, the Baron walked over and picked up the paper with the message on it.

His eyes gleamed.

Taking out his snuff box he took a large pinch, then put the snuff box — and Nicholas's note — in his pocket.

He gave a wicked smile, thinking it was a fine evening for hunting an heiress. And one as beautiful as Miss Julianne Appleby was fortunate indeed. He would have to tread carefully though, as he had been informed she was no fool.

Although only a foolish young lady would meet her lover far away from the ballroom on a moon-lit evening.

It was his lucky night. It should be easy to capture and compromise Miss Appleby and so secure her wealth. Her didn't care a fig about her, of course, but once she'd married him he would then be able to get what he wanted from her.

He practically ran out of the ballroom into the garden, making a footmen stare at his haste.

7

Aunt Bridget was delighted to be told the news that Julianne was going to have a private tête-à-tête with her nephew. 'It's about time!' she exclaimed under her breath. But her joy became concern when she thought about where they were to meet. 'Oh, my,' she cried as she looked out of the windows, 'it's becoming dark out there.'

Orangeries were not like conservatories, attached to a house; they were separate from the main house, situated in the garden. And the ball they were attending was in a very large house with an even bigger garden.

'Take Jack with you,' she called after Julianne's retreating figure. But even though Julianne turned to acknowledge the instruction she'd been given, Aunt Bridget had the feeling the girl was too intent on meeting her lover to think about her safety.

Aunt Bridget rose immediately from her seat where she'd been sitting with the older ladies and began to look for Jack.

He was easy to spot because of his bright yellow coat and white breeches among the rest of the men who wore the conventional evening dress of a dark blue coat and cream knee breeches.

'Jack, Jack, come here at once!' Her shrill command penetrated her nephew's brain, although he'd drunk far too much that evening to understand her deep concern.

Obediently and good-naturedly, he came tottering over to his aunt with a glass in one hand and a bottle of wine in the other. 'I'm here, Aunt, at your command,' he said with a grin.

Aunt Bridget could see at once that he was incapable of finding anything, especially the quick-footed Julianne, who would be at least halfway to the orangery by now.

She would have to go and look for

her charge herself. But she would need the assistance of some reliable gentleman. She looked around the assembly and spied Major Wilmot, who was an old friend of her late husband. She practically ran over to him and explained the situation in stilted little gasps.

'Take my arm, your ladyship, and I'll escort you to the orangery. I know the garden reasonably well,' he said gallantly.

'Do hurry, major,' urged Aunt Bridget.

'M'am,' the major exclaimed, 'I ain't a young man any longer. Got a gammy leg fighting with Wellington, don't you know. But we'll gallop along as best we can. Can't see the gel will come to any harm with Featherstonhaugh though. I believe he's a sound young fella — no matter what scandal has recently been spread about him.'

★   ★   ★

The grand house where the ball was taking place that evening had an equally grand and enormous garden surrounding it. Acres of cultivated ground that contained mature trees and an orderly arrangement of lawns, walks and flower-beds, as well as a walled kitchen garden, and at the height of the summer it looked its best.

Julianne wasn't sure where the orangery was but she knew she was looking for a large ornate greenhouse. The trouble was there were no signs to say where all the paths went to after she'd left the ballroom and stepped outside into the darkening light of the garden.

There would be no friendly gardeners about she could ask at this time of night and even the blazing lights from the house gave her little indication of where to go. It was a moonlit night however, which helped.

She realised she should have taken Aunt Bridget's advice and asked Jack to accompany her. Not that he would know the layout of the garden any more than she did but a least she wouldn't be a young lady out alone without an escort.

In her haste, she hadn't even had the wit to ask a footman which direction she should go to find the building she was looking for, which she knew wasn't wise and her mama would faint with shock if she knew she had ventured out alone. But her mama was probably safely tucked up in bed at the moment so she wouldn't lose any sleep over her reckless behaviour.

She hummed to herself as she walked first down one path, then another, hoping she would soon find the orangery.

At the end of a grove of trees she came across a small temple. Turning another way she saw a large garden shed, no doubt where the gardeners stored their tools. Then, beginning to worry about the time it was taking her to find the orangery, Julianne quickened her step.

But which way should she go? The huge garden was beginning to feel like being in a maze.

She must have been at least a quarter of an hour walking here and there and not finding any building that looked like a large hothouse. She heard an owl hoot and wished it was Nicholas calling her. Where is Nicholas? Will he give up waiting for me? How dim-witted I am not to have asked someone where the orangery was before I left the ballroom!

After another quarter of an hour searching in the dim evening light, Julianne was relieved to hear the crunch of a man's boots on the gravel path coming towards her.

'Nicholas!' she cried, relieved and delighted he'd found her.

But it was not Nicholas who came striding down the path. It was a gentleman she did not wish to meet. Coming towards her was the worst of men. Julianne had learned after two Seasons the kind of men who were to be avoided and here was a prime example of one: Baron Percy Browne.

Oh, dear! What shall I do?

Being out alone in the garden at night was against the rules for young ladies and for the practical reason that unaccompanied girls became easy prey for men like Baron Browne. No doubt he would try to appear charming, offer to escort her to wherever she wanted. But it would be words only. He would have in mind to dishonour her and then demand she marry him because he was a fortune-hunter who wanted not her, but her money.

She turned and ran only to find her path took her towards a grotto.

It was a dead end and her heart practically stopped like her steps.

Anxious but determined to keep control of her rising panic, Julianne breathed deeply. Her fashionable white gown didn't make it easy for her to hide but hide she must, because if she were to be cornered by the baron the consequences would be fatal. And after her silliness of encouraging other suitors, which had been observed by others beside Nicholas, no one would have sympathy for whatever might befall her.

Julianne had to make a quick decision. *What can I do to hide from him?*

After a few moments looking around the grotto and nearby shrubs and trees, her despair at finding no place to hide resulted in her checking the trees, looking for one to clamber up to be out of sight.

I know it is unladylike to shin up a tree — but needs must.

Selecting the nearest oak tree with low study branches, her hoyden youth came in useful. She ignored the unsuitability of her muslin dress, which would get torn, as she pulled herself up onto the lowest branch, then stepped up onto a higher one and up again. Soon she was panting with fright as much as the physical effort she needed to climb the tree and hide herself amongst the leafy branches.

Perhaps I should climb a little higher just in case the wretched man happens to look upwards?

After she'd climbed up as high as she dare, she clung to the rough bark of the tree trunk and peered down through the leaves to see the baron had arrived beneath her, looking around to see where she'd gone.

She was repulsed to hear him calling her in his hissing voice, 'Pretty Sugar Plum, I am here to find you and kiss you!'

Sugar Plum indeed! Julianne almost fell out of the tree in disgust. His sentiment was false. His intentions, she was well aware, were dishonourable.

When he called again after searching for her, 'I can see you,' Julianne almost fell out of her hiding place up in the tree. Her beating heart almost stopped in panic. But she began to realise that it was a lie, just like the many he then went on to say, trying to entice her to show herself.

If anything made Julianne cower

more, it was the realisation that she had brought this disaster upon herself and that brought tears into her eyes. It had been her own decision to encourage attention from men and, especially as she was supposed to be engaged, she'd confused many men into thinking she was a flighty miss. Perhaps Baron Browne thought so, too.

Now she was paying the price of her own folly.

Not hearing any more calls for a while, Julianne hoped the baron had looked around and, not seeing her, he had gone off to look elsewhere. But how did she know he wasn't playing a cat and mouse game and was lying in wait for her to reveal where she was?

Anyway, she couldn't appear in public with a torn dress and covered in dozens of small scratches over the arms and shoulders. What would people think she had been up to? Not climbing a tree that was for sure!

She began to feel the prickly branches irritate her skin and a trickle of blood from a scratch had bled a little, staining her white dress with a small, bright red patch.

Even clinging onto the rough tree soon became unpleasant. But even more alarming was the fact that she began to wonder if she would even be able to get down!

Her face perspired, her hands too, which made them slippery on the branch she grasped.

Looking down, although there was no sign of the baron, it seemed a very long way down to the ground.

I will fall and hurt myself badly — or even be killed! She sobbed as she thought of the ridiculousness of her current predicament — and that in her silliness, she had brought it all upon herself.

★ ★ ★

Meanwhile the Earl of Featherstonhaugh was suffering too.

He had paced up and down the

orangery many times. He'd gone outside the hothouse to look along the path, expecting to find his beloved coming to see him, going over in his mind what he wanted to say to her.

Although he would never consider to eat humble pie and ask for forgiveness for having her ring in his pocket, especially when it had been she who had sent it to him, but, as Aunt Bridget had made clear to him, he might lose her if he didn't make some conciliatory gesture by giving her back her ring and ending their argument, accepting the fact that she was but a female, liable to faults, and had to appear to win arguments at times.

Although, he thought to himself, Julianne must not think that she would always be able to manipulate him thus — and he would certainly make that clear when he saw her.

No more dallying with other men when she was married to him. But in his heart he knew she had only made a show of flirting in order to be defiant and he was convinced she really loved him and would be true to him after this matter was settled.

But time was getting on now. Where was she?

Guilt struck Nicholas as he suddenly realised he shouldn't have asked her to meet him in the garden. It was folly — and he shouldn't have suggested it. No wonder she hadn't come, because a sensible girl like Julianne would certainly have known better than to sally forth, alone and unescorted, out into the huge garden at night.

With a troubled heart Nicholas walked back towards the house, wondering now how he was to approach Julianne with a reasonable excuse as to why he'd expected her to meet him in such an unsuitable place. He hoped to find her dancing merrily and he expected her to either ignore him, or to receive a look of disapproval from her.

What he didn't expect was to be confronted with disapproval from his

Aunt Bridget as soon as he stepped into the ballroom.

'Where is Julianne?' demanded his aunt.

Nicholas shrugged, 'I don't know, Aunt.'

His aunt could have shrieked but she was too well-bred, and merely cut him deeply with a look that was fully intended to hurt, She said icily. 'Find her immediately! She went out into the garden to look for you an hour ago after receiving your message to meet her in the orangery.'

Nicholas stared at his aunt in horror. He had no answer to that. He had to take immediate action.

He marched into the card room and, taking Jack by his bright coloured collar, he dragged him to a quiet corner of the room.

'Hey! What's the matter, Nicholas?' spluttered Jack.

Nicholas couldn't blame Jack for Julianne's disappearance and gulped down his anger. 'Julianne is missing,' he managed to say, without giving Jack a bloody nose. 'She's somewhere in the garden and you must help me find her immediately.'

Jack scratched his head. 'Don't ask me where your fiancée is Nicholas. She ain't my responsibility.'

Nicholas knew this to be true. He had to keep on the right side of Jack if he wanted his help, even though he smelled strongly of drink. 'Listen, you and I used to play in this garden when we were young. You know the layout as well as I do. So, please, come and help me search the garden. I really must find her and quickly.'

'What's she doing out there?'

'Because I asked her to meet me in the orangery.'

Jack, although overfilled with wine, had the greatest difficulty not to chuckle and take the opportunity to tell his elder brother what an idiot he was. So often he'd had to put up with Nicholas telling him off so he would have loved to have called his older brother a goose. But he refrained from doing so and managed to keep a straight face. Besides, he liked Julianne and offered to do what he could to help.

'Please go and collect Aunt Bridget and organise some footmen to send out a search party. But do it calmly, for heaven's sake, we don't everyone here to know she's lost. There is already more than enough tittle-tattle surrounding her as it is.'

Jack could see his brother was truly worried and nodded. 'I will send the cavalry to the rescue,' he quipped in his half-drunken state.

But Nicholas had already turned around and was marching, not too fast, in case anyone should suspect something was amiss, out into the garden.

He had been to the duke's house many times in his youth and in fact he knew the layout of the place pretty well. It was just a case of figuring out where to look for Julianne first.

He asked a footman who was

standing near the open French windows if he'd noticed a young lady leave the ball and go out into the garden about an hour or so ago.

The footman looked at the Earl with a stony face. 'I can't say what time it was she left, Sir, but I did notice that Baron Browne standing on the terrace at the time and that he went off after her, and he hasn't come back yet.'

The worst possible thought crossed Nicholas's mind as he marched out into the dimly lit garden.

When he was out of sight of the house, he began to run as fast as he could and his heart pounded.

How could he have been so short-sighted? So sure of his own version of why Julianne was at fault about the ring, he'd overlooked the most important aspect — her safely.

And now he'd thoughtlessly put her in danger!

8

Meanwhile Julianne was clinging to the rough surfaced tree trunk for dear life. Feeling more insecure and uncomfortable by the minute, and worried she might slip and fall off the tree, her brow was shining with perspiration and her hands had become wet and slippery.

She tried again to get down onto the lower branch in the same manner as she had gotten up but she now realised that climbing up a tree was far easier than getting down it.

She prayed as she'd never prayed before. She felt convinced she would fall and that there would be no one to find her eventually — after all, who would know she was up here in the oak tree? Even Aunt Bridget had expected her to go to the orangery, not to be stuck up a tree near the grotto.

Julianne envisaged the gardeners

finding her body lying at the foot of the tree in the morning. She shuddered, thinking of all the beetles and snakes that might be lurking in the garden, and other wild animals who might find her there and crawl all over her!

Time must be getting on. What would Nicholas be thinking of her not coming to find him?

She put her head against the rough bark and felt the tears run down her cheeks. She was in a hopeless situation!

Then she heard someone calling loudly, 'Julianne!'

Her ears pricked. She heard it again. Yes, she was sure it was someone calling her. But was it Baron Browne?

After a few minutes she no longer heard the person calling her.

Should she have replied?

Agonies of wondering if she had lost her only chance to he saved assailed her. What if it had been Baron Browne — what harm could he do her up a tree? Anyway he had called her 'sugar plum', hadn't he? But the voice calling her name hadn't, so it couldn't have been the baron.

It was not long afterwards that she heard her name being called again. 'Julianne, where are you?'

She knew immediately who was calling her this time — it was her beloved Nicholas. Her heart leapt with joy. But her throat was dry as she tried to call back to him and nothing but croaks escaped her lips. Terrified he might not hear her, she tried desperately to shout louder so he could, 'Nicholas!'

His calling had stopped. Perhaps he hadn't heard her efforts to call his name, so she tried shouting, 'I'm here!' and making any sound she could to attract his attention. But as there was no response from him she knew he must have gone away.

It became a nightmare for Julianne. Her fingernails clinging onto the bark and ivy with such ferocity that part of the ivy gave way and she slipped. She screamed as she felt herself falling but she somehow managed to grasp another small branch. Now she found herself almost upside down and stuck in the fork of the tree.

How long could she cling on before falling? But looking down she saw Nicholas's concerned face looking up at her.

'What the hell are you doing up there?' he boomed, unable to hide his relief at having found her but cross that she had been found in such an indelicate position.

'Help me,' she said weakly, 'I can't get down.'

Oh, dear me — Nicholas was clearly in a fix. She could tell he was wondering if he should run for assistance or scramble up the tree before she fell out of it altogether.

'Hang on. I'm coming up.'

He'd chosen to climb up to be with her and she felt so relieved. She watched him take off his evening coat which he threw on a nearby shrub, then he looked up to decide which was the best route to take as he rubbed his strong hands together. Having decided, he swung himself up onto the lowest tree limb and from there began to climb higher, calling as he scrambled up, 'I'll be with you in a minute.'

Huffing and puffing, because he'd been running around the garden looking for her for some time already now, Nicholas slowly clambered up the tree towards her.

'Oh, I was so frightened,' Julianne said, as her fear somewhat ebbed away when she saw him climbing easily up the branches.

'Just hold on, Julianne, whatever you do.'

'I can't hold on much longer. I've already been up here for so long.'

'Well, don't fall on me now, there's a good girl.'

She giggled, even though she still had tears in her eyes. The whole situation was a farce. Never in her wildest dreams did she expect a thing like this to happen.

But she wasn't surprised Nicholas was an expert climber, nor that he was taking it all in good humour. Which was just as well because she felt exceedingly embarrassed stuck at such an awkward angle up in a tree.

It wasn't long before he was near her, assessing her situation. 'Mmm,' she heard him say, 'how did you get yourself in such a tangle?'

Despite having her frilly pantaloons on show, which was bad enough, Julianne was mortified to find she couldn't think of a way to right herself.

'I slipped,' she gasped, more exasperated with herself than him for asking her how she managed to get herself in such an dangerous position.

He managed to give her a quick kiss on the cheek. 'Well now, do as I say and we'll soon set you aright.'

'I do hope so.'

He instructed her as if he was teaching her a new dance. 'First you must put your right hand further along the branch towards the tree trunk.'

'I don't think I can. I'll slip off.'

'Yes you can. You won't fall, because I'm going to hold you.'

'I'm too heavy for you to hold. You'll fall, Nicholas.'

'No we won't. I'm firmly wedged and I can take your shoulders as you move your hand.'

Julianne realised she had to trust him to support her but she felt afraid to let go of her grip in case she fell. 'Nicholas,' she whispered, 'I dare not.'

'You can trust me to hold you, can't you?'

She could but she still needed the courage to let go of the branch. Her heart leapt into her throat as she glanced down at the earth, such a long way down beneath her.

He was becoming impatient. 'Julianne, get on with it. I'll say, one, two, three and then you must move your hand.'

Julianne hated having to lose control of her body and allow Nicholas to carry her, even for a few seconds, but she knew she couldn't stay as she was for much longer without falling. She trusted him to hold her; she just had to show it.

She closed her eyes tightly, listened to him chanting the numbers, and then she let go . . .

Next minute she was surprised to find herself sitting upright again on a sturdy branch, and Nicholas had clambered up beside her and had his arm around her already.

'There, there,' he said soothingly in his deep, comforting voice. 'You're quite safe now.'

Using his pocket handkerchief to pat her face, she said, 'How will we ever get down onto the ground? I'll never manage.'

'Of course you will. But have a little rest first. Lean against me.'

Julianne liked the sensation of being seated so close and supported by the man she loved. She thought that is how it should have been all the Season, if she hadn't been so silly, trying to make him jealous by dallying with other men.

Yet, was it all her fault?

He made no attempt to say more and let her cling to his warm body. But after a while he asked, 'Tell me why you are up here?'

'I wanted to hide. Baron Browne was after me. I couldn't think how to get away from him. So I climbed this tree.'

'Very wise!' Nicholas was trying not to laugh, doing his best to see the serious side of the predicament Julianne had found herself in. 'The Baron is a menace to young ladies, especially those who possess a fortune. But I think it wasn't necessary for you to have climbed up quite so high.'

'I was afraid he might see me and come after me.'

'Ah.'

'I know it was stupid of me to have got so far from the ground.'

'My dear girl, it was not your fault you had to disappear from view. It was my fault for asking you to meet me in the orangery in the first place — and at night-time, too. I just didn't think and I am sorry to have got you in this position. But I'll make sure you are safe and sound with your feet on the ground very soon.'

'I'm so afraid, Nicholas,' she said, her voice trembling. 'When I look down I have the feeling I'm about to fall.'

'Then don't look down, my love. Look at me and I shall look into your beautiful eyes and keep you safe.'

And so she did, although in the dark she could only see the glitter from his eyes but she thought them exquisite nonetheless.

He suddenly gave a chuckle.

'What's so amusing?'

'Us, being stuck up a tree. How strange life can be!'

Julianne smiled a little too. 'I'll feel more amused about it when I'm standing on the ground. I'm quite exhausted.'

He snuggled her closer. 'Well don't feel tempted to move yet. I have to work out exactly how we are going to climb down safely together. In the meantime I want to tell you something.'

'Yes, Nicholas?'

'I wanted to see you tonight to put and end to our disagreements. To admit I have your ring . . . '

'You have? Oh, Nicholas that's wonderful! Let me have it please! I promise I won't ever take it off again.'

'Unfortunately, I put it in my jacket pocket and I left that on the bush there, just under the tree.'

'Then I will look forward to having your exquisite ring on my finger again once we get to the ground.'

'Does this mean you are still willing to marry me?'

She put her arm around him and squeezed him, saying, 'Of course I love you and want to marry you, Nicholas! It was naughty of me not to tell you before when you asked me. And to make such a fuss over our missing correspondence too — can you ever forgive me?'

'My dearest, we can all be at fault at times. So let us just rejoice that we have found contentment together — even here, up in a tree!'

Julianne shuffled over and snuggled as close as she could to him and felt she was truly in heaven.

They sat in companionable silence and heard a cuckoo calling as it flew by, heralding that morning was approaching. Soon after came the dawn chorus as blackbirds begin singing their sweet sounding tunes, too.

It was, Julianne realised, a magical moment for her. She was not quarrelling with Nicholas anymore and they were in harmony, like the birds up in the trees. It was unreal for her to be out at this time, alone with a man, but then their whole relationship had been somewhat unusual. But what did it matter? They were together again at last.

'Do you hear people coming?' She had fallen asleep a little earlier and Nicholas awoke her gently.

She listened sleepily. 'Yes, I do,' she replied, 'it sounds like there are many people coming.'

'It's about time. I organised a search party for you hours ago.'

'Goodness me! Are people looking for me?'

'Of course they are. Aunt Bridget was concerned that you ran out into the garden unchaperoned.'

'Oh dear! She'll be cross with me.'

'We are both in her bad books, I fear.'

Sure enough as the group appeared below them, Aunt Bridget's somewhat croaky voice was to be heard calling, 'Julianne!'

'I'm here.'

'Where? Where are you?'

'My poor aunt, she's almost lost her voice calling you. I'll call back,' Nicholas said and Julianne was pleased he'd warned her as his very loud shout to attract his aunt's attention almost made her lose her balance.

Before long his aunt was under the tree looking up at them. 'What on earth are you doing up there in the boughs, Nicholas?'

'I'm making sure Julianne isn't going to fall down, Aunt.'

'Do you mean to tell me you have Julianne up there as well?'

'Yes, indeed. She's quite safe.'

Aunt Bridget was obviously lost for words, or her voice had become so lacking in strength she had difficulty in replying, but she did eventually manage to croak, 'Well, get the gel down at once!'

'Easier said than done. We are quite high up here.'

'What madness to take her up there!'

Nicholas gave a chuckle, 'She got herself up here in the first place, Aunt. I only went up to get her down. Please, would you ask a footman to get a ladder to help get her down? She's a little apprehensive about the descent and needs some assistance.'

'Well I never! You and your brother must be the stupidest men on earth! Jack! Jack, come here! Now, look up that tree where I'm pointing. The Earl of Featherstonhaugh has got himself and his fiancée stuck up there. Don't ask me how, I don't pretend to understand you two boys or the follies you get up to. But I want Julianne down this instant. I really don't care about what happens to your brother, he can stay up there forever, for all I care . . . ' her voice had petered out.

Jack came to stare up at them saying, 'Right-ho, Aunt. Never fear — I've summoned the fire brigade.'

Nicholas groaned, 'Now everyone in London will know we are up here.'

But Julianne really didn't mind because they were there together.

Underneath them they heard Aunt Bridget discussing his rescue plan.

'Please be serious, Jack. There isn't a fire.'

'True, Aunt, but firemen are very good at throwing ladies over their shoulder and carrying them down ladders. There was a fire in the mews last month and I watched them save several people like that.'

Their voices faded as they walked

away and left Julianne and Nicholas.

'I would really rather you got me down,' said Julianne, not fancying being slung over a fireman's shoulder like a bag of coal.

'Well, you've had a good rest, so it should be easier for you. Just do as I say, and I'll steady you.'

She had to be brave. But she trusted Nicholas and she really longed to be down on the solid earth again.

He slid off the branch onto a lower one and told her to wriggle forward so that she could do the same.

'Hold my hands,' he said, holding out his hands to take hers. He looked secure as he propped himself firmly against the tree trunk. With her feet dangling in the air it seemed a long gap before they were finally on the lower branch, but she gritted her teeth and left her perch to make the little jump down to where Nicholas was.

They wobbled a bit as she landed beside him. But he held her tightly and she gave a little laugh of relief.

'Now, walk sideways toward me a few steps — put your hands on my shoulders to steady yourself — then I'm going to step down to the next branch and I want you to step down with me.'

It was surprising simple to make the next move and Julianne felt quite pleased with herself when they both arrived safely on the sturdy branch, even though they dislodged a few small twigs and leaves on the way.

'There,' said Nicholas, 'you got up and now you are getting down and have got over the worse part. Well done!'

Julianne felt triumphant. 'If I realised it was going to be so simple I would have done it hours ago,' she said.

Nicholas grunted, 'I'm glad you didn't try. You could have fallen.'

Then she felt ashamed of the trouble she had caused and said quite humbly, 'I wouldn't have been able to get down without your help Nicholas.'

'Nor get up without Baron Browne on your heels, eh?'

'Indeed not. I never climb trees

— well, at least not nowadays,' she said, abashed. 'Not since I was a child.'

Nicholas chuckled. 'I should hope not. Adventures like this are best left to boys — and hoyden girls.'

The last part of their descent was easy.

Nicholas got down on the ground first and, holding her waist, he lifted her down. Once her feet were safely on the ground he held her crushed against him. 'Now please, don't do that again. You might not have been frightened — but you certainly frightened me!'

She was too content just to cling to him to say anything about how scared she had really been.

They were not left alone for long. An army of footmen came running along with ladders and looked dismayed to see the couple had already got down.

Nicholas still held onto Julianne's hand as he faced them and apologised for the trouble he'd caused them, before sending them away again.

But when the fire engine arrived with

a loud clanging bell and they were surround by firemen, Julianne whispered to Nicholas, 'We must make sure they get paid for their trouble. I feel utterly ashamed to have been the one to have caused all this furore.'

'It was my fault,' Nicholas assured her, 'I started it all by summoning you to come into the garden. I'll have to go and apologise to our host too. But before that I have something else I must do.'

Julianne didn't care everyone there was watching him take her in his arms and kiss her passionately.

'Let's forget about our past correspondence, shall we?' she suggested between their kisses. 'Who wrote to whom last doesn't matter really.'

'All forgotten,' he whispered in her ear. 'And, as you now know, I've found your ring.'

'That's splendid!' She nuzzled closer to him, not thinking to ask how or where it was found. All that mattered was that the impediments between them had vanished into thin air on this magical night.

Before long Aunt Bridget appeared again, accompanied by a bevy of maids and hustled Julianne away and into her coach.

'Only one thing of good has come out of all this,' Aunt Bridget managed to croak. 'There is no getting out of marrying Nicholas now. You have truly compromised yourself.'

Even with a torn and ruined muslin dress and scratches all over her arms, legs and face, Julianne was still able to smile.

Nicholas, she notice, turned to wave and blow her a kiss to her before she rode off in the coach.

Then she turned her attention to her Godmother who looked completely exhausted by it all. 'My dear Lady Bridget, I can't thank you enough for making us finally see sense,' she said.

But the dear lady's eyes were already closed as she slumped back on to the carriage cushions.

However, Julianne's own tiredness had vanished.

She felt alert and alive with a curious tingling — and a longing for Nicholas to kiss her again as he'd just done. She felt sure they had both been frightened of losing one another that night, and had now reached an agreement to marry and let bygones be bygones.

The evening had not gone to plan — far from it — but as far as she was concerned it had been a brilliant success.

9

It was early morning by the time Nicholas returned to his house, tired but in a state of happiness to be reconciled with Julianne. He slept for several hours but, when he awoke, he was shocked. He remembered he'd left his jacket — with her ring inside the pocket — on a shrub in the duke's garden!

He felt annoyed with himself and anxious. Could his jacket still be there where he'd left it? Had anyone picked it up? And would anyone have noticed the valuable ring and taken it?

His previous encounter with the portly Duke of Chubb, having to apologise, hadn't been pleasant, because the duke hadn't a sense of humour, and didn't see the amusing side of his guests climbing trees.

The duchess, who'd been kept up

until the early hours too, was not smiling while the hue and cry had gone on about her missing guest, Miss Julianne Appleby. And then she was furious when a fire-engine had run over their lawn making ghastly wheel marks, and frightening the peacocks.

The severe looking duchess had made a particularly cutting remark that Nicholas was a disgrace to the aristocracy with his wild ways and that his brother, Jack, with their Follies Hotel, was certainly no better either.

The Earl of Featherstonhaugh, who had been jacketless and his cravat askew, as well as having various small tears on his clothes to show for his tree-climbing antics, could only agree that his behaviour had been regrettable and apologised again.

'You won't be invited here again,' the duke had mumbled as he'd followed the duchess, walking away after her to retire.

So Nicholas had bowed at their retreating backs and had left them with his tail between his legs, determined never to visit their house again.

But now, in the morning, he realised he'd have to.

He needed his ring to give it back to Julianne. Yes, he needed that ring today, he couldn't have another like it made. Besides Julianne would know it was not the same ring. He didn't want to offend her again. He longed to visit her as soon as he could, taking the ring with him.

Having shaved and bathed, he informed his valet, Murray, 'I'm not going to eat any more humble pie and beg that haughty duke to be allowed to search in his garden for my jacket.'

Murray, seeing how tetchy his master seemed that morning, could only agree with him.

'You have many other jackets, m'lord,' the valet reminded him.

'I know, but the one I left behind last night has something in the pocket that is of great value to me.'

The long-suffering Murray, who had

only just been able to get back to normal when the Follies Hotel crowd had moved out of the Earl's town house, sighed. But as he liked the young Earl, he offered to go and get the jacket for him.

'No, I'll have to fetch it myself, thank you. Only I know exactly where it is to be found. You don't know where the grotto is in that vast garden, or which bush I left it on.'

The valet bowed, 'No, m'lord. I'm not an outdoors servant and confess I'm not familiar with gardens.'

While Murray was busily tying Nicholas's cravat, Nicholas suddenly shouted, 'Stop!'

The man stopped immediately and stepped back apprehensively.

Nicholas said. 'I have an idea! Do you know where I might find some gardener's clothing?'

'Well,' the surprised valet replied, 'I could ask our gardeners.'

'Then do so, if you please. I intend to borrow some workman's clothes to wear so that I can slip into the duke's garden and find my jacket myself. Anyone who sees me will think I'm just a gardener.'

'Unlikely, my lord.'

'Well I must go,' Nicholas went on, 'Now see what you can obtain for me to wear while I have some breakfast.'

As his valet had foreseen, the Earl of Featherstonhaugh looked nothing like an ordinary run-of-the-mill gardener when he was dressed up as one. Some members of the aristocracy might be disguised very well, but not Nicholas, whose impressive figure and confident air was all too apparent.

★　★　★

Scaling the high wall surrounding the Duke of Chubb's massive property wasn't something Nicholas found easy. First he looked around to make sure no one was around to see him. Then he leaped up and grasped the wall with both hands and slowly hauled himself to sit on the top of the wall.

Feeling quite proud of himself, he jumped down the other side and began to stride through the undergrowth to find his bearings as if he owned the place. And he only just managed to avoid a nasty looking man-trap.

But he didn't manage to avoid a sharp-eyed gamekeeper.

'Hoi! You there. Come 'ere, or I'll shoot you.'

Appalled, Nicholas turned to see the leather-gaited gamekeeper with his gun pointing at him.

It was a heart-stopping moment. Should he run for it and risk being shot?

Nicholas decided he'd better put his hands up.

He was taken at gun-point into the breakfast room to where the Duke and Duchess of Chubb were having brunch.

'He says he's an Earl of something,' stated the gamekeeper giving Nicholas a prod with his rifle barrel.

Nicholas received stony looks from

both the duke and the duchess.

'You may leave him here, Smith, I know perfectly well who this fellow is.'

After the gamekeeper left the room, the only noise Nicholas heard was the duke slurping his coffee, and the duchess crunching her toasted muffin. So he waited patiently.

'So what have you got to say for yourself this time, Featherstonhaugh?'

Feeling like an errant schoolboy, Nicholas said, 'I came to get my jacket I left here last night.'

'Most visitors come to the front door and ring the bell,' remarked the duchess dryly.

'I appreciate that, ma'am. But I didn't want to disturb you. I thought that by dressing in my gardener's clothes I might sneak in and retrieve my jacket without bothering anyone.'

The duke snorted, 'What is it about your family that they have to behave in such vulgar ways? Your father lost all his money gambling, I've heard the rumour going round that you have turned your town house into a hotel with a shady reputation, and now I discover you creeping around my gardens, climbing trees with young ladies and dressed up like a gardener!'

The duchess piped up in a scandalised tone, 'What would your dear, late mama think of your behaviour? She was always so respectable. We noble families are expected to set standards, you know, to be courteous, and not behave like ruffians.'

Nicholas thought the duke and duchess were not exactly charming people either, but he replied, 'Our family is as respectable as any other, sir. In fact we have every reason to rejoice our troubles are over. My papa's debts have been paid off, my brother has moved his hotel from my town house to another and it is thriving. And I am engaged to marry the sweetest girl in the world, Julianne Appleby, who as I'm sure you are aware, has a great fortune of her own.'

Both the duke and duchess looked at him in amazement.

'You mean you are no longer short in the pocket?'

Nicholas nodded. 'I never was that short, my lord. Gossips tend to make a bad situation seem worse than it is.'

Seeing he had scored well, Nicholas continued, 'I came here to collect my jacket because I had put Julianne's ring in the pocket of it and, naturally, she wants it back.'

Neither the duke nor the duchess could argue with that.

'Well . . . er . . . I . . . ' stuttered the Duke of Chubb, 'We'd better get someone to search for your coat and bring it here, I suppose.'

Nicholas bowed. 'I used to play here with your son as a boy, my lord, so I know the layout of your garden well. May I suggest you allow me to find my jacket, then I'll be off with it and out your life forever.'

The Duke of Chubb rose to his feet, dabbed his mouth with his napkin, and said, 'There's no need for that I hope, Featherstonhaugh. When you are married I dare say you and your wife will fit into Society nicely. So you must not be offended over this incident and obliged to cut us in future.'

Nicholas considered he had every reason to want to avoid seeing the top-lofty noble Chubbs in the future but he knew the higher ranks in Society were few in number and it was better for them to remain on polite speaking terms. So he managed to bow, and say, 'No indeed, my lord. I bear you no ill will. In fact, I've never been to a better party than yours last night.'

'But for now, with your kind permission, I'll be off to pick up my jacket. Please be kind enough to ask your staff to ignore me so I don't get captured again.' He gave another low bow, 'Good day to you, ma'am.'

The duchess forced a smile, 'You must come again, Featherstonhaugh — and do feel free to climb more of our trees if you wish.'

'I don't think my future wife will permit it.'

They all chucked and parted on good terms.

But as soon as Nicholas strode into the garden he began to worry about being so independent about saying he would find his jacket. What if his jacket was not there where he'd left it? What if a gardener, or indeed a real poacher, had already walked off with it?

10

Julianne felt quite sore in places when she awoke. Then she remembered her adventure of the night before and smiled dreamily, knowing that it was well worth the battle wounds, because Nicholas was her loving fiancé once again.

When her dressing maid told her the time she was a little worried. Morning visits were over by twelve and it was almost midday. Had Nicholas called and she'd been asleep in bed? She hoped not.

Taking care to choose a day dress which covered her scratched arms, she asked her maid to arrange her hair so that some locks fell over a bruise on her cheek and a small cut at the side of her nose.

Looking pretty in her lilac, flowered gown she tripped downstairs with a smile on her lips — until she heard women's voices that sounded as if they were quarrelling. One of the voices she recognised was her mama's. Glory be! What had brought her here!

Stopping on the lower steps of the stairs, Julianne wondered what she should do and decided to listen first before she went barging into the room.

Mrs Appleby was scolding Aunt Bridget quite loudly. 'I expected you to escort Julianne to dances not allow her to climb trees.'

'Clara, I did not give her permission to do anything of the sort! She told me she had to get away from an undesirable gentleman and she was doing the only sensible thing she could do when she climbed that tree.'

'Sensible? Do you call that sensible? Well, I do not, Bridget! She has not yet fully grown out of her childish, hoyden ways. She must come home with me today and I will teach her how to behave like a lady ought to.'

'Mind you, I think it is all the fault of

that Earl of Featherstonhaugh. She was quite well behaved until she met him. He's nothing but a money seeking scoundrel.'

'Clara! Nicholas is no scoundrel. You are talking about my dear brother's son. My brother may have been a spend-thrift — he liked horse-racing far too much — but neither he, nor his sons, are rogues. All of his debts have been paid back in full due to the hard work and careful housekeeping of the Earl ever since he took over from his father. I really do think Nicholas is rather to be congratulated than berated.'

'Not so, Bridget. He has ruined my daughter's reputation.'

'I think not! Julianne climbed the tree first. Nicholas merely went up to fetch her down. Would you have preferred he walked away like a coward and didn't rescue her?'

'He didn't rescue her.'

'He did.'

Mrs Appleby snorted. 'I was told the fire brigade had to be called.'

'So it was — a little late, however, as Julianne was already safely on the ground by then, assisted by Nicholas.'

Julianne's mouth twisted into a smile, as she continued to listen to the ding-dong verbal battle between her mama and Godmother.

'Nevertheless, I'm taking Julianne home. Today. This very minute, in fact. I have the coach waiting for us outside. I never want her to see, or hear about, the owner of the Follies Hotel again.'

Julianne gasped so loudly she was afraid her mama might hear.

But just at that moment, the door bell sounded and soon after a well attired young gentleman was ushered into the drawing room. Bowing to Mrs Appleby and to his aunt, Jack — whose outrageous dandy clothes had been replaced, by more respectably sensible attire — said, 'Did I hear you mention the owner of the Follies Hotel, ma'am? I am the owner.' He smiled at Mrs Appleby proudly.

'You are not the owner,' contradicted

Mrs Appleby. 'The Earl of Featherston-haugh owns the property. Everyone who is anyone knows that is so, because I was the one who put it about.'

Julianne's eyes blinked fast several times.

'Ma'am,' Jack said with the utmost politeness, 'With the greatest respect, my brother Nicholas was never the Follies Hotel owner. He hasn't got the business acumen that I have to run it successfully. I own one of the foremost hotels in London and it is no longer in my brother's house. I have moved premises to a new place I bought myself.'

Mrs Appleby was wide eyed.

'The Prince of Wales himself comes to my hotel, ma'am. His Royal Highness has given me permission to change the name of the Follies Hotel and call it The Royal Hotel. He advised me where to find a good tailor so that I can look the part of a first class hotelier.'

'The Prince — do you mean the

Prince of Wales comes to your hotel?'

'Frequently, ma'am. He likes the décor Julianne helped me choose, and our chef's food. The Prince is a good humoured fellow, don't you know, and we get on extremely well.'

Mrs Appleby was clearly impressed to discover a new step for her to climb up the social ladder. None other than the Prince Regent! She would be able to crow about this to her friends; knowing someone who was friends with royalty!

Julianne too was intrigued to hear all this — and to see Jack attired as a well-turned out young gentleman, someone who had met the Prince Regent — that she couldn't stop herself from coming nearer the drawing room door. There she stood and gaped seeing Jack's transformation from a dandy to a man of discernment in his dress and manner.

He looked almost as handsome as her fiancé.

Jack continued, 'Ma'am. I hate to

contradict a beautiful lady, but what would my brother, Nicholas, want with an hotel? He is quite rich enough with the estates he has, as well as his fine town house.'

Mrs Appleby was now in awe of the charming young gentleman and smiled at him, hoping to gain some royal news to tell her friends back home. And Jack, Viscount Milverton, was well practiced at charming his hotel guests — even somewhat hostile ones.

'Yes, ma'am,' he went on as Clara clearly seemed unable to say anything, 'I hear plenty of gossip, especially amongst the higher echelons of Society, but I don't believe all the tittle-tattle I hear. You don't, do you? No, I should think not!'

Julianne couldn't help a giggle escape her lips, making her mother's attention turn to her. 'Julianne, my dear child.' She didn't rise to hug her daughter but asked, 'Are you in good health?'

Julianne went forward to kiss her mama saying, 'Of course I am. A little tree climbing has brought me down to earth. I have never been happier.'

'Good,' said her mama cautiously, 'then we shall go home before anything else untoward happens to you.'

Julianne knew everything she wanted depended on her now. She had to delay her mother's departure. She had to wait for Nicholas to come and reaffirm his desire to marry her.

She knew her mama had annoyed kind Aunt Bridget and the two ladies would not be friends again for some time, unless she could think of something to make her mother change her mind.

Jack had certainly done his best to explain to her mother about his Follies Hotel being only temporarily in Nicholas's town house.

If only Nicholas would come soon.

Julianne feared she might have mistaken his desire to marry her. He didn't need her wealth and could marry any pretty girl he chose without taking on a mother-in-law like Mrs Appleby.

Her heart pounded painfully. She racked her brains for something to say that would delay her mother insisting that she be whisked away.

It was Jack who saved the day again. 'Ladies, my hotel is nearby and I have the best chef in London waiting to serve you. May I invite you to luncheon? I expect you are ready for something tasty to eat as you had a very early start from your home, dear Mrs Appleby.'

'Now tell me what your favourite dish is — perhaps a side of beef with frizzled potatoes? Or a roasted goose? And I know you ladies enjoy fruit cream tarts so I'll send word for a meal to be prepared for you.'

Mrs Appleby huffed. 'I don't know that your hotel is for respectable ladies. I'm told it is full of undesirable pictures and art objects.'

'Indeed it is not, Mama,' Julianne said sharply. 'Jack has new furnishings, which I helped him to choose, and I helped him to select the decorating as well. And I thought of you when I was choosing every picture, statue and all the furnishings. They are all in the best of taste and everything is of the finest quality.'

Mrs Appleby was clearly staggered. 'Well bless my soul!' she exclaimed and sat fanning her face.

Aunt Bridget was the next to speak. 'There now, my dear Clara, you see that your fears are unfounded. The ton's prattle is way off mark. My nephew has learned from his youthful mistakes, haven't you, Jack?'

Jack bowed. 'Indeed. Julianne is a fine teacher. She has given me good guidance in what is the best.'

'And that is because you taught me to be discerning, Mama,' cried Julianne. 'You showed me how to feel fabrics for their quality as well as to choose them for their quality and colour.'

Her mother looked pleased.

'Do come along to the Royal Hotel, ma'am,' said Jack, offering Mrs Appleby his arm. 'I was thinking as you are a lady of good taste, you may like to see it for yourself.'

Mrs Appleby seemed to be flattered and was just about to rise to her feet, when she asked suddenly, 'And where is the Earl of Featherstonhaugh?'

Everyone looked at each other. Julianne was aghast while Aunt Bridget simply shrugged.

'Here I am!' the Earl announced himself as he strode into the room, with a wide grin on his face.

But everyone — especially Mrs Appleby — looked shocked.

'Why are you dressed like that?' demanded Aunt Bridget, looking at his dishevelled gardener's clothes.

'My, oh my!' exclaimed Mrs Appleby, sitting down again and raising her gloved hands in horror. 'Is there no end to your nephew's outrageous conduct, Lady Bridget?'

Julianne was simply too pleased to see Nicholas to care what he was wearing, and skipping over to him, stood on her toes and gave him a kiss.

Mrs Appleby was about to protest, but Nicholas got in first. 'Forgive my attire, ladies. I had to climb over the Duke of Chubb's estate wall this morning searching for my jacket because I had put Julianne's ring in the pocket of it. I had to retrieve it so that I could return it to her.' He held the ring up to sparkle in his fingers.

'You've got my ring! Nicholas, how wonderful you are!'

He kissed her and, taking her hand, slipped the ring on her finger as Julianne squealed with delight.

After kissing Julianne, Nicholas turned to her mother and said, 'Now my ring is where it should be, Mrs Appleby. And it was exceeding wrong of you to send Julianne's ring back to me as you obviously did.'

Mrs Appleby became pale, looking almost frightened, hearing Nicholas's powerful accusation.

There was a sharp intake of breath from everyone in the room.

The Earl continued, 'Yes, I have given the matter much thought and came to the conclusion that you, Mrs Appleby, took the ring from Julianne's bedchamber without her knowing about it, and posted it to me without a note of explanation.'

Mrs Appleby's deceit being exposed clearly shamed her for she sat looking decidedly uncomfortable.

'Mama! How could you!' cried Julianne.

Nicholas's arm squeezed Julianne gently to his body as he continued, 'My poor girl has been most upset about it — and so was I. And I dare say it was you also, Mrs Appleby, who stopped our correspondence because, as I told Julianne, I continued to write to her for a long time even after she stopped writing to me.'

'Mama!' shrieked Julianne. 'Your behaviour has been dreadful. Fancy stealing Nicholas's letters! They meant so much to me. It hurt me deeply to lose them. And you knew all the time what had happened to them as I searched everywhere!'

'I thought I was doing it for your good, child.' Clara Appleby had the grace to look ashamed.

'You mean, your good, Mama. Because you didn't want me to marry a man you thought would ruin your chances of gaining prestige amongst your friends. Well, Mama, there's no question of me coming home with you now. I have nothing to learn about good behaviour from you! I want to stay here.'

Nicholas turned to look at Julianne, saying, 'Do you want me, my love?'

Julianne smiled at him, 'I do.'

'And you will marry me as soon as I can arrange it?'

'I will, Nicholas, as you know perfectly well. You are the man I love. Shall we travel the world together, as we talked about, before we settle down at Featherstonhaugh Hall?'

Mrs Appleby had become pale and opened her mouth to say something, but nothing came out.

'Well, that was truly disgraceful of you, Clara!' Lady Bridget declared.

There was a murmur of agreement in the room.

'However,' Lady Bridget continued, 'we're not going to say any more about the follies we have all got up to in the past few months! Things have been said and done, that shouldn't have been. Society has had much to gossip about us. But that is all over now and we shall show them that it was all a bumble-broth — as I said it was in the beginning.'

She went up to Julianne and kissed her, then stood on tip-toe to kiss her tall nephew, and said. 'These two love birds are perched together again which is all that really matters, so come along, Clara, and enjoy your luncheon at the Royal Hotel. We must discuss their wedding breakfast.'

Mrs Clara Appleby seemed only too pleased to have her transgressions forgiven so rapidly and trotted off with

Lady Bridget and Jack.

Julianne and Nicholas lingered behind when everyone had left.

'You can't go to the Royal Hotel for lunch dressed like that,' said Julianne looking at his clothes. 'You are more suited for being in a garden.'

'I agree. Shall we have a picnic in the garden?'

'What a lovely idea, Nicholas! But to tell the truth, I'm not very hungry.'

Nicholas chuckled, 'Neither am I, my sweet. Shall we simply go for a stroll in the garden, eh?'

'Yes, indeed,' said Julianne with a cheeky smile on her lips, 'especially as Mama and my godmother are not around . . . '

THE END

We do hope that you have enjoyed reading this large print book.

Did you know that all of our titles are available for purchase?

We publish a wide range of high quality large print books including:
Romances, Mysteries, Classics
General Fiction
Non Fiction and Westerns

Special interest titles available in large print are:
The Little Oxford Dictionary
Music Book, Song Book
Hymn Book, Service Book

Also available from us courtesy of Oxford University Press:
Young Readers' Dictionary
(large print edition)
Young Readers' Thesaurus
(large print edition)

For further information or a free brochure, please contact us at:
Ulverscroft Large Print Books Ltd.,
The Green, Bradgate Road, Anstey,
Leicester, LE7 7FU, England.
Tel: (00 44) **0116 236 4325**
Fax: (00 44) **0116 234 0205**

Other titles in the
Linford Romance Library:

WHEN WORDS GET IN THE WAY

Wendy Kremer

Rebecca works for a PR company organising the forthcoming centenary celebrations of Daniel Seymour's company. Although a successful businessman, Daniel struggles to accept that, as a divorcee, he has failed at marriage. Whilst Rebecca, after her parents' divorce, shies away from emotional commitment, not wanting history to repeat itself. Although from different worlds, they are both independent and wary. Will they move in the right direction — or be carried off-course by their own uncertainties?